Critical Acclaim for the Incomparable Queen of Suspense and #1 *New York Times* Bestselling Author MARY HIGGINS CLARK and *MY GAL SUNDAY*

"Tantalizing . . . Fans of Nick and Nora 'Thin Man' movies . . . will fall in love with Mary Higgins Clark's newest detective team. Readers will hope there will be many more tales about them. A great treat . . ."

—Harriet Klausner, *Bookpage*

"These adventures are in keeping with Ms. Clark's more humorous fiction, such as her tales of the inimitable Willy and Alvirah. . . . Henry and Sunday . . . offer comic relief. . . ."

—Ann Lloyd Merriman, *Richmond Times-Dispatch*

"The romance of wealth . . . [is] coupled . . . with the potent fairy-tale mix of power, glamor, [and] gentility . . . in this gentle, upscale epithalamion."

—*Kirkus Reviews*

Books by Mary Higgins Clark

My Gal Sunday
Moonlight Becomes You
Silent Night
Let Me Call You Sweetheart
The Lottery Winner
Remember Me
I'll Be Seeing You
All Around the Town
Loves Music, Loves to Dance
The Anastasia Syndrome and Other Stories
While My Pretty One Sleeps
Weep No More, My Lady
Stillwatch
A Cry in the Night
The Cradle Will Fall
A Stranger Is Watching
Where Are the Children?

Published by POCKET BOOKS

MARY HIGGINS CLARK

My Gal Sunday

POCKET BOOKS

New York   London   Toronto   Sydney   Tokyo   Singapore

POCKET BOOKS, a division of Simon & Schuster Inc.
1230 Avenue of the Americas, New York, NY 10020

ISBN: 0-671-01491-9

First Pocket Books printing November 1997

10 9 8 7 6 5 4 3 2 1

POCKET and colophon are registered trademarks of
Simon & Schuster Inc.

Cover art by Tom Hallman

Printed in U.S.A.

Acknowledgments

As a child I had frequent attacks of asthma. The reward for a night of gasping for breath was that in the morning, when the attack eased, I'd be propped up in bed with books and a radio.

At regular intervals I'd tune in to a number of radio dramas, those great old continuing sagas which invited me to share glamorous adventures.

My favorite by far was *Our Gal Sunday.* The pitch for it went something like this: "The story that asks the question 'Can a girl from a mining town in the West find happiness as the wife of England's richest, most handsome lord, Lord Henry Brinthrop?' "

I had a huge crush on Lord Henry and thought he and Sunday were a perfect couple. *Yes,* she could find happiness with him. Who couldn't, for heaven's sake?

That was why, when I wanted to create a new husband-and-wife suspense team, I thought about Lord Henry and Sunday and asked myself, "Suppose Henry is a former American president, smart, nice, rich, and gorgeous? Suppose Sunday is a stunning, savvy young congresswoman?" These stories are the result. I hope you enjoy them.

They wouldn't have evolved without the guidance, nurturing, encouragement, and wisdom of my longtime editor,

Michael Korda, and his associate, senior editor Chuck Adams. Again, as always, thank you, guys—I love you. Multiple thanks to Gypsy da Silva, copy editor incomparable, patience personified.

Richard McGann of Vance Security in Washington, D.C., a former Secret Service agent, has been my valued expert in explaining the Secret Service protection a former president and his wife would experience. Detective Sergeant Kevin J. Valentine of the Bernardsville, New Jersey, Police Department willingly answered all my many questions about the procedure that would be followed if a child were suddenly to be found seemingly abandoned. Thank you, thank you, Dick and Kevin.

Finally, as always, blessings and thanks to my family and friends, who cheer me on as I approach deadlines and patiently understand my tunnel vision when I'm immersed in tales to be told. You're all the greatest!

For John
with love
à tout jamais

Contents

_____

My Gal Sunday

A Crime of
Passion

◆

"'Beware the fury of a patient man,'" Henry Parker Britland IV observed sadly as he studied the picture of his former secretary of state. He had just learned that his close friend and political ally had been indicted for the murder of his lover, Arabella Young.

"Then you think poor Tommy did it?" Sandra O'Brien Britland said with a sigh as she patted homemade jam onto a hot scone, fresh out of the oven.

It was still early morning, and the couple was comfortably ensconced in their king-sized bed at Drumdoe, their country estate in Bernardsville, New Jersey. *The Washington Post, The Wall Street Journal, The New York Times, The Times* (London), *L'Osservatore Romano,* and *The Paris Review,* all in varying stages of being read, were scattered about, some lying on the delicately flowered, gossamer-soft quilt, others spilling over onto the floor. Directly in front of the couple were matching breakfast trays, each complete with a single rose in a narrow silver vase.

"Actually, no," Henry said after a moment, slowly shaking his head. "I find it impossible to believe. Tom always had such strong self-control. That's what made him such a fine secretary of state. But ever since Constance died—it was during my second administration—he just hasn't seemed himself. And it was obvious to everyone that when he met Arabella he just fell madly in love. Of course, what also became obvious after a while was that he had lost some of that steely control—I'll never forget the time he slipped and called Arabella 'Poopie' in front of Lady Thatcher."

"I do wish I had known you then," Sandra said ruefully. "I didn't always agree with you, of course, but I thought you were an excellent president. But then, nine years ago, when you were first sworn in, you'd have found me boring, I'm sure. How interesting could a law student be to the president of the United States? I mean, hopefully you would have found me attractive, but I know you wouldn't have taken me seriously. At least when you met me as a member of Congress, you thought of me with some respect."

Henry turned and looked affectionately at his bride of eight months. Her hair, the color of winter wheat, was tousled. The expression in her intensely blue eyes somehow managed to convey simultaneously intelligence, warmth, wit, and humor. And sometimes also childlike wonder. He smiled as he remembered the first time he met her: he had asked if she still believed in Santa Claus.

That had been the evening before the inauguration of his successor, when Henry had hosted a cocktail party at the White House for all the new members of Congress.

"I believe in what Santa Claus represents, sir," Sandra had replied. "Don't you?"

Later, as the guests were leaving, he had invited her to stay for a quiet dinner.

"I'm so sorry," she had replied. "I'm meeting my parents. I can't disappoint them."

Left to dine alone on this final evening in the White House, Henry had thought of all the women who over the past eight years had readily changed their plans in a fraction of a second, and he realized that at last he had found the woman of his dreams. They were married six weeks later.

At first the media hype threatened to be unending. The marriage of the country's most eligible bachelor—the forty-four-year-old ex-president—to the beautiful young congresswoman, twelve years his junior, set off a feeding frenzy among journalists. Not in years had a marriage so completely captured the public's collective imagination.

The fact that Sandra's father was a motorman on the New Jersey Central Railroad, that she had worked her way through both St. Peter's College and Fordham Law School, spent seven years as a public defender, then, in a stunning upset, won the congressional seat of the longtime incumbent from Jersey City, already had made her a champion to womankind, as well as a darling of the media.

Henry's status as one of the two most popular presidents of the twentieth century, as well as the possessor of a considerable private fortune, combined with the fact that he appeared with regularity at or near the top of the list of America's sexiest men, made him likewise a favorite source of copy, as well as an object of envy by other men who could only wonder why the gods so obviously favored him.

On their wedding day, one tabloid had run the headline: LORD HENRY BRINTHROP MARRIES OUR GAL SUNDAY, a reference to the once wildly popular radio soap opera that daily, five days a week, for years on end, asked the question: "Can a girl from a mining town in the West find happiness as the wife of England's richest and most handsome lord, Lord Henry Brinthrop?"

Sandra had immediately become known to one and all, including her doting husband, as Sunday. She hated the nickname at first, but became resigned to it when Henry pointed out that for him it had a double meaning, that he thought of her as "a Sunday kind of love," a reference to the lyrics of one of his favorite songs. "Besides," he added, "it suits you. Tip O'Neill had a nickname that was just right for him; Sunday is just right for you."

This morning, as she studied her husband, Sunday thought back over the months they had spent together, days that until this morning had remained almost carefree. Now, seeing the genuine concern in Henry's eyes, she covered his hand with hers. "You're worried about Tommy. I can tell. What can we do to help him?"

"Not very much, I'm afraid. I'll certainly check to make sure the defense lawyer he has hired is up to the task, but no matter who he gets to represent him, the prospects look bleak. Think about it. It's a particularly vicious crime, and when you look at the circumstances it's hard not to assume that Tom did it. The woman was shot three times, with Tommy's pistol, *in* Tommy's library, right after he told people how upset he was that she had broken up with him."

Sunday picked up one of the papers and examined the picture of a beaming Thomas Shipman, his arm around the dazzling thirty-year-old who had helped to dry his tears following his wife's death. "How old is Tommy?" Sunday asked.

"I'm not sure. Sixty-five, I'd guess, give or take a year."

They both studied the photograph. Tommy was a trim, lean man, with thinning gray hair and a scholarly face. In contrast, Arabella Young's wildly teased hair framed a boldly pretty face, and her body possessed the kind of curves found on *Playboy* covers.

"A May-December relationship if I ever saw one," Sunday commented.

"They probably say that about us," Henry said lightly, forcing a smile.

"Oh, Henry, be quiet," Sunday said. Then she took his hand. "And don't try to pretend that you aren't really upset. We may still be newlyweds, but I know you too well already to be fooled."

"You're right, I am worried," Henry said quietly. "When I think back over the past few years, I can't imagine myself sitting in the Oval Office without Tommy at my side. I'd only had one term in the Senate before becoming president and in so many ways I was still very green. Thanks to him I weathered those first months without falling on my face. When I was all set to have it out with the Soviets, Tommy—in his calm, deliberate way—showed me how wrong I'd be to force a confrontation but then publicly managed to convey the impression that he was only a sounding board for my own decision. Tommy is a true statesman, but more to the point, he is a gentleman, through and through. He's honest, he's smart, he's loyal."

"But surely he's also a man who must have been aware that people were joking about his relationship with Arabella and just how smitten he was with her? Then when she finally wanted out, he lost it," Sunday observed. "That's pretty much the way you see it, isn't it?"

Henry sighed. "Perhaps. Temporary insanity? It's possible." He lifted his breakfast tray and put it on the night table. "Nevertheless, he was always there for me, and I'm going to be there for him. He's been allowed to post bond. I'm going to see him."

Sunday quickly shoved her tray aside, barely managing to catch her half-empty coffee cup before it spilled onto the quilt. "I'm coming too," she said. "Just give me ten minutes in the Jacuzzi and I'll be ready."

Henry watched his wife's long legs as she slid out of bed. "The Jacuzzi. What a splendid idea," he said enthusiastically. "I'll join you."

Thomas Acker Shipman had tried to ignore the army of media camped outside, near his driveway. When he and his lawyer pulled up in front of his house, he had simply stared straight ahead and barged his way from the car to the house, desperately trying not to hear the roar of questions hurled at him as he passed. Once inside, however, the events of the day finally hit him, and he visibly slumped. "I think a scotch may be in order," he said quietly.

His attorney, Leonard Hart, looked at him sympathetically. "I'd say you deserve one," he said. "But first, let me once again reassure you that if you insist, we'll go ahead with a plea bargain, but I'm compelled to once more point out to you that we could put together a very strong insanity defense, and I wish you'd agree to go to trial. The situation is so clear that any jury could understand: you went through the agony of losing a beloved wife, and on the rebound you fell in love with an attractive young woman who at first accepted many gifts from you, then spurned you. It is a classic story, and one that I feel confident would be received sympathetically when coupled with a temporary insanity plea."

As he spoke, Hart's voice became increasingly passionate, as though he were addressing a jury: "You asked her to come here and talk it over, but she taunted you and an argument ensued. Suddenly, you lost your head, and in a blinding rage so intense that you can't even remember the details, you shot her. The gun normally was kept locked away, but this evening you had it out because you had been so upset that you actually had entertained thoughts of killing yourself."

The lawyer paused in his presentation, and in the moment of silence the former secretary of state stared up at him, a puzzled look on his face. "Is that actually how you see it?" he asked.

Hart seemed surprised at the question. "Why, yes, of course," he replied. "There are a few details we have to iron out yet, a few things that I'm not completely clear on. For example, we'll have to explain how you could simply leave Miss Young bleeding on the floor and go up to bed, where you slept so soundly that you didn't even hear your housekeeper's scream when she discovered the body the next morning. Based on what I know, though, I would think that at the trial we would contend that you were in a state of shock."

"Would you?" Shipman asked wearily. "But I wasn't

in shock. In fact, after I had that drink, I just seemed to start floating. I can barely remember what Arabella and I said to each other, never mind recalling actually shooting her."

A pained look crossed the lawyer's face. "I think, Tom, that I must beg you not to make statements like that to anyone. Will you promise me, please? And may I also suggest that certainly for the foreseeable future you go easy on the scotch; obviously it isn't agreeing with you."

Thomas Shipman stood behind the drapes as he peered through the window, watching as his rotund attorney attempted to fend off a charge by the media. Rather like seeing the lions released on a solitary Christian, he thought. Only in this case, it wasn't Attorney Hart's blood they were after. It was his own. Unfortunately, he had no taste for martyrdom.

Fortunately, he had been able to reach his housekeeper, Lillian West, in time to tell her to stay home today. He had known last evening, when the indictment was handed down, that television cameras would be camped outside his house, to witness and record every step of his leaving in handcuffs, followed by the arraignment, the fingerprinting, the plea of innocence, and then this morning's less-than-triumphal return home. No, getting into his house today had been like running the gauntlet; he didn't want his housekeeper to be subjected to that too.

He did miss having someone around, though. The house felt too quiet, and lonely. Engulfed by memories, his mind was drawn back to the day he and Constance had bought the place, some thirty years ago. They had driven up from Manhattan to have lunch at the Bird and Bottle near Bear

Mountain, then had taken a leisurely drive back to the city. Impulsively, they had decided to detour through the lovely residential streets in Tarrytown, and it was then that they came across the For Sale sign in front of this turn-of-the-century house overlooking the Hudson River and the Palisades.

And for the next twenty-eight years, two months, and ten days, we lived here in a state of happily ever after, Shipman thought. "Oh, Constance, if only we could have had twenty-eight more," he said quietly as he headed toward the kitchen, having decided on coffee instead of scotch as the drink he needed.

This house had been a special place for them. Even when he served as secretary of state and had to travel so much of the time, they managed to have occasional weekends together here, and always it was a kind of restorative for the soul. And then one morning two years ago, Constance had said, "Tom, I don't feel so well." And a moment later she was gone.

Working twenty-hour days had helped him numb the pain somewhat. *Thank God I had the job to distract me,* he thought, smiling to himself as he recalled the nickname the press had given him, "The Flying Secretary." *But I not only kept busy; Henry and I also managed to do some good. We left Washington and the country in better shape than it's been in for years.*

Reaching the kitchen, he carefully measured out enough coffee for four cups and then did the same with the water. *See, I can take care of myself,* he thought. *Too bad I didn't do more of it after Constance died. But then Arabella entered the scene. So ready with comfort, so alluring. And now, so dead.*

He thought back to the evening, two days ago. What *had* they said to each other in the library? He vaguely remembered becoming angry. But could he actually have been angry enough to carry out such a terrible act of violence? And how could he possibly have left her bleeding on the library floor while he stumbled up to bed? He shook his head. It just didn't make sense.

The phone rang, but Shipman only stared at it. When the ringing stopped, he took the receiver off the hook and laid it on the counter.

When the coffee was ready, he poured a cup and with slightly trembling fingers carried it into the living room. Normally he would have settled in his big leather chair in the library, but not today. Now he wondered if he would ever be able to enter that room again.

Just as he was getting settled, he heard shouting from outside. He knew the media were still encamped on his street, but he couldn't imagine the cause of such a racket. Yet before he even pulled back the drapes far enough to allow him to peer outside, he had guessed what had caused the furor.

The former president of the United States had arrived on the scene, to offer friendship and comfort.

The Secret Service personnel tried valiantly to clear a path for the Britlands as they forged their way through the crowd of reporters and cameramen. With his arm protectively around his wife, Henry paused, indicating his willingness to offer at least a cursory statement: "As always in this great country, a man is innocent until proven guilty. Thomas Shipman was a truly great secretary of state and remains a close friend. Sunday and I are here today in friendship."

Having made his statement, the former president turned and headed toward the porch, ignoring the barrage of questions the reporters hurled at him. Just as they reached the top step leading to the porch, Tom Shipman unlocked and opened the front door, and his visitors glided inside without further incident.

It was only when the door had closed behind the Britlands, and he felt himself enclosed in a firm and reassuring bear hug, that Thomas Shipman began to sob.

Sensing that the two men needed some time to talk privately, Sunday headed to the kitchen, insisting against Shipman's protest that she prepare lunch for the three of them. The former secretary kept saying that he could call in his housekeeper, but Sunday insisted that he leave everything to her. "You'll feel a lot better when you have something in your stomach, Tom," she said. "You guys say your hellos and then come join me. I'm sure you must have everything I need to make an omelet. It'll be ready in just a few minutes."

Shipman, in fact, quickly regained his composure. Somehow just Henry Britland's presence in his home gave him the sense, at least for the moment, that he could handle whatever it was that he would have to face. They went to the kitchen, finding Sunday already at work on the omelet. Her brisk, sure movements at the chopping board brought back for Shipman a recent memory of Palm Beach, and of watching someone else prepare a salad, while he dreamed of a future that now could never be.

Glancing out the window, he realized suddenly that the shade was raised, and that if somebody managed to sneak around to the back of the house, there would be a perfect opportunity to snap a candid photo of the three of them. Swiftly, he moved across the room and lowered the shade.

He turned back toward Henry and Sunday and smiled sadly at the two of them. "You know, I recently got talked into putting an electronic setup on the drapes in all the other rooms, something that would let me close them either by a timer or by a mere click of the control. I never thought I'd need that in here, though. I know almost nothing about cooking, and Arabella wasn't exactly the Betty Crocker type herself."

He paused and shook his head. "Oh, well. It doesn't matter now. And besides, I never did like the damn things. In fact, the drapes in the library still don't work right. Every time you click to either open or close them, you get this loud cracking noise, almost like somebody firing a gun. Oddly appropriate, wouldn't you say? I mean, since there really was a gun fired in there less than forty-eight hours ago. You've heard about events casting their shadows before them? Well . . ."

He turned away for a moment, the room silent except for the sounds of Sunday getting the omelet ready for the pan. Then Shipman moved to the kitchen table and sat across from Henry. He was reminded almost immediately of the times they had faced each other across the desk in the Oval Office. He looked up, catching the younger man's eye. "You know, Mr. President, I—"

"Tommy, knock it off. It's me. Henry."

"All right, Henry. I was just thinking that we are both lawyers, and—"

"And so is Sunday," Henry reminded him. "Don't forget. She did her time as a public defender before she ran for office."

Shipman smiled wanly. "Then I suggest that she's our resident expert." He turned toward her. "Sunday, did you ever have to launch a defense where your client had been dead drunk at the time the crime was committed, in the course of which he not only shot his . . . ah . . . friend, three times, but left her sprawled out on the floor to bleed to death while he staggered upstairs to sleep it off?"

Without turning from the stove, she responded. "Maybe not quite those circumstances, but I did defend a number of people who had been so high on drugs at the time that they didn't even remember committing the crime. Typically, though, there were witnesses who offered sworn testimony against them. It was tough."

"So they were found guilty, of course?" Shipman asked.

Sunday paused and looked at him, smiling ruefully. "They had the book thrown at them," she admitted.

"Exactly. My attorney, Len Hart, is a good and capable fellow who wants me to plead guilty by reason of insanity —temporary, of course. But as I see it, my only course is to plea bargain in the hope that in exchange for a guilty plea, the state will not seek the death penalty."

Henry and Sunday now both were watching their friend as he talked, staring straight ahead. "You understand," Shipman continued, "that I took the life of a young woman who ought to have enjoyed fifty years more on this planet. If I go to prison, I probably won't last more than five or ten years. The confinement, however long it lasts, may help to expiate this awful guilt before I am called to meet my Maker."

All three of them remained silent as Sunday finished

preparing the meal—tossing a salad, then pouring beaten eggs into a heated skillet, adding chopped tomatoes, scallions, and ham, folding the ends of the bubbling eggs into flaps, and finally flipping the omelet over. The toast popped up as she slid the first omelet onto a heated plate and placed it in front of Shipman. "Eat," she commanded.

Twenty minutes later, when Tom Shipman pushed the last bit of salad onto a crust of toast and stared at the empty plate in front of him, he observed, "It is an embarrassment of riches, Henry, that with a French chef already employed in your kitchen, you are also blessed with a wife who is a culinary master."

"Thank you, kind sir," Sunday said briskly, "the truth is, whatever talents I have in the kitchen began during the time I put in as a short-order cook when I was working my way through Fordham."

Shipman smiled as he stared distractedly at the empty plate in front of him. "It's a talent to be admired. And certainly one Arabella didn't possess." He shook his head slowly from side to side. "It's hard to believe I could have been so foolish."

Sunday put her hand on top of his, then said quietly, "Tommy, certainly there have got to be some extenuating circumstances that will work in your favor. You've put in so many years of public service, and you've been involved in so many charitable projects. The courts will be looking for anything they can use to soften the sentence—assuming, of course, that there really is one. Henry and I are here to help in any way we can, and we will stay by your side through whatever follows."

Henry Britland placed his hand firmly on Shipman's shoulder. "That's right, old friend, we are here for you.

Just ask, and we will try to make it happen. But before we can do anything, we need to know what really did happen here. We had heard that Arabella had broken up with you, so why was she here that night?"

Shipman did not answer immediately. "She just dropped in," he said evasively.

"Then you weren't expecting her?" Sunday asked quickly.

He hesitated. "Uh . . . no . . . no, I wasn't."

Henry leaned forward. "Okay, Tom, but as Will Rogers said, 'All I know is just what I read in the papers.' According to the media accounts, you had phoned Arabella earlier in the day and begged her to talk to you. She had come over that evening around nine."

"That's right," he replied without explanation.

Henry and Sunday exchanged worried glances. Clearly there was something that Tom wasn't telling them.

"What about the gun?" Henry asked. "Frankly, I was startled to hear that you even had one, and especially that it was registered in your name. You were such a staunch supporter of the Brady Bill, and were considered an enemy by the NRA. Where did you keep it?"

"Truthfully, I had totally forgotten I even had it," Shipman said tonelessly. "I got it when we first moved here, and it had been in the back of my safe for years. Then coincidentally I noticed it there the other day, right after hearing that the town police were having a drive to get people to exchange guns for toys. So I just took it out of the safe and had left it lying on the library table, the bullets beside it. I had planned to drop it off at the police station the next morning. Well, they got it all right, just not in the way I had planned."

Sunday knew that she and Henry were sharing the same thought. The situation was beginning to look particularly bad: not only had Tom shot Arabella, but he had loaded the gun after her arrival.

"Tom, what were you doing before Arabella got here?" Henry asked.

The couple watched as Shipman considered the question before answering: "I had been at the annual stockholders' meeting of American Micro. It had been an exhausting day, exacerbated by the fact that I had a terrible cold. My housekeeper, Lillian West, had dinner ready for me at seven-thirty. I ate only a little and then went directly upstairs because I still wasn't feeling well. In fact, I even had chills, so I took a long, hot shower; then I got into bed. I hadn't been sleeping well for several nights, so I took a sleeping pill. Then I was awakened—from a very sound sleep, I must say—when Lillian knocked on my door to tell me that Arabella was downstairs to see me."

"So you came back downstairs?"

"Yes. I remember that Lillian was just leaving as I came down, and that Arabella was already in the library."

"Were you pleased to see her?"

Shipman paused for a moment before answering. "No, I was not. I remember that I was still groggy from the sleeping pill and could hardly keep my eyes open. Also I was angry that after ignoring my phone calls, she had simply decided to appear without warning. As you may remember, there is a bar in the library. Well, Arabella already had made herself at home by preparing a martini for both of us."

"Tom, why would you even think of drinking a martini on top of a sleeping pill?" Henry asked.

"Because I'm a fool," Shipman snapped. "And because I was so sick of Arabella's loud laugh and irritating voice that I thought I'd go mad if I didn't drown them out."

Henry and Sunday stared at their friend. "But I thought you were crazy about her," Henry said.

"Oh, I was for a while, but in the end, I was the one who broke it off," Shipman replied. "As a gentleman, though, I thought it proper to tell people that it had been her decision. Certainly anyone looking at the disparity in our ages would have expected it to be that way. The truth was, I had finally—*temporarily,* as it turns out—come to my senses."

"Then why were you calling her?" Sunday asked. "I don't follow."

"Because she had taken to phoning me in the middle of the night, sometimes repeatedly, hour upon hour. Usually she would hang up right after hearing my voice, but I knew it was Arabella. So I had called her to warn her that it couldn't go on that way. But I certainly did *not* invite her over."

"Tom, why haven't you told any of this to the police? Certainly based on everything I have read and heard, everyone thinks it was a crime of passion."

Tom Shipman shook his head sadly. "Because I think that in the end it probably was. That last night Arabella told me that she was going to get in touch with one of the tabloids and was going to sell them a story about wild parties that you and I allegedly gave together during your administration."

"But that's ridiculous," Henry said indignantly.

"Blackmail," Sunday said softly.

"Exactly. So do you think telling that story would help

my case?" Shipman asked. He shook his head. "No, even though it wasn't the case, at least there's some dignity to being punished for murdering a woman because I loved her too much to lose her. Dignity for her, and, perhaps, even a modicum of dignity for me."

Sunday insisted on cleaning up the kitchen while Henry escorted Tommy upstairs to rest. "Tommy, I wish there were someone staying here with you while all this is going on," the former president said. "I hate to leave you alone."

"Oh, don't worry, Henry, I'm fine. Besides, I don't feel alone after our visit."

Despite his friend's admonition, Henry knew he would worry, as he began to do almost immediately after Shipman went off to the bathroom. Constance and Tommy had never had children, and now so many of their close friends from the area had retired and moved away, most of them to Florida. Henry's thoughts were interrupted by the sounding of his ever-present beeper.

Using his cellular phone, he replied immediately. The caller was Jack Collins, the head of the Secret Service team assigned to him. "I'm sorry to bother you, Mr. President, but a neighbor is most anxious to get a message to Mr. Shipman. She says that a good friend of his, a Countess Condazzi who lives in Palm Beach, has been trying to get through to him, but he is not answering his phone and apparently his answering machine is turned off, so she has been unable to leave him a message. I gather that she has become somewhat distraught and is insisting that Mr. Shipman be notified that she is awaiting his call."

"Thanks, Jack. I'll give Secretary Shipman the message. And Sunday and I will be leaving in just a few minutes."

"Right, sir. We'll be ready."

Countess Condazzi, Henry thought. How interesting. I wonder who that can be?

His curiosity deepened when, on being informed of the call, Thomas Acker Shipman's eyes brightened, and a smile formed on his lips. "Betsy phoned, eh?" he said. "How dear of her." But almost as quickly as it had appeared, the brightness faded from his eyes, and the smile vanished. "Perhaps you could send word to my neighbor that I won't be accepting calls from anyone," he said. "At this juncture, there seems to be little point in talking to anyone other than my lawyer."

A few minutes later, as Henry and Sunday were being hustled past the media, a Lexus pulled into the driveway next to them. The couple watched as a woman jumped from the car and, using the stir created by their departure as diversion, managed to get to the house undisturbed, where, using her own key, she entered immediately.

"That has to be the housekeeper," Sunday said, having noted that the woman, who appeared to be in her fifties, was dressed plainly and wore her hair in a coronet of braids. "She certainly looks the part, and besides, who else would have a key? Well, at least Tom won't be alone."

"He must be paying her well," Henry observed. "That car is expensive."

On the drive home, he told Sunday about the mysterious phone call from the countess in Palm Beach. She made no comment, but he could tell from the way she tilted her head to one side and puckered her forehead that she was both disturbed and deep in thought.

The car they were riding in was a nondescript, eight-year-old Chevy, one of the specially equipped secondhand cars Henry kept available for their use, especially helpful in allowing them to avoid detection when they so desired. As always, they were accompanied by two Secret Service agents, one driving while the other rode shotgun. A thick glass divider separated the front seat from the back, allowing Henry and Sunday the freedom to talk without being overheard.

Breaking what for her was an extended silence, Sunday said, "Henry, there's something wrong about this case. You could sense it from the accounts in the paper, but now, having talked to Tommy, I'm certain of it."

Henry nodded. "I agree completely. At first I thought that perhaps the details of the crime might be so gruesome that he had to deny them even to himself." He paused, then shook his head. "But now I realize that this is not a question of denial. Tommy really doesn't know what happened. And all of this is just so unlike him!" he exclaimed. "No matter what the provocation—threats of blackmail or whatever—I cannot accept that even confounded by the combination of a sleeping pill and a martini, Tommy could go so completely out of control as to have killed the woman! Just seeing him today made me realize how extraordinary all this is. You didn't know him then, Sunday, but he was *devoted* to Constance. Yet when she died, his composure was remarkable. He suffered, yes, but he remained calm throughout the entire ordeal." He paused, then shook his head again. "No, Tommy simply isn't the kind of man who flips out, no matter what the provocation."

"Well, his composure may have been remarkable when his wife died, but then falling hook, line, and sinker for Arabella Young when Connie was barely cold in her grave does say something about the man, you'll have to agree."

"Yes, but rebound perhaps? Or denial?"

"Exactly," Sunday replied. "Of course, sometimes people fall in love almost immediately after a great loss and it actually works out, but more often than not, it doesn't."

"You're probably right. The very fact that Tommy never married Arabella after actually giving her an engagement ring—what, nearly two years ago?—says to me that almost from the outset he must have known it was a mistake."

"Well, all of this took place before I came on the scene, of course," Sunday mused, "but I did keep abreast of much of it through the tabloids, which at the time made a big fuss over how in love the staid secretary of state was with the flashy PR person only half his age. But then I remember seeing two photos of him run side by side, one showing him out in public, snuggling Arabella, while the other was taken at his wife's burial and obviously caught him at a moment when his composure had slipped. No one that grief stricken could be that happy only a couple of months later. And the way she dressed—she just didn't seem to be Tommy's kind of woman."

Sunday sensed rather than saw her husband's raised eyebrow. "Oh, come on. I know you read the tabloids cover to cover after I'm done with them. Tell me the truth. What did you think of Arabella?"

"Truthfully, I thought of her as little as possible."

"You're not answering my question."

"I try never to speak ill of the dead." He paused. "But if you must know, I found her boisterous, vulgar, and obnoxious. She possessed a shrewd enough mind, but she talked so fast and so incessantly that her brain never seemed able to keep up with her mouth. And when she laughed, I thought the chandelier would shatter."

"Well, that certainly fits in with what I read about her," Sunday commented. She was silent for a moment, then turned to her husband. "Henry, if Arabella really was stooping to blackmail with Tommy, do you think it is possible she had tried it before, with someone else? I mean, is it possible that between the sleeping pill and the martini, Tommy passed out, and someone else came in without him knowing it? Someone who had followed Arabella, and who suddenly saw an opportunity to get rid of her and let poor Tommy take the blame?"

"And then carried Tommy upstairs and tucked him into bed?" Henry again raised an eyebrow.

They both fell silent as the car turned onto the approach to the Garden State Parkway. Sunday stared out the window as the late afternoon sunshine turned the trees, with their copper and gold and cardinal red leaves, aglow. "I love autumn," she said pensively. "And it hurts to think that in the late autumn of his life, Tommy should be going through this ordeal." She paused. "Okay, let's try another scenario. You know Tommy well. Suppose he was angry, even furious, but also was so groggy that he couldn't think straight. Put yourself in his position at that moment: what would you have done?"

"I would have done what Tommy and I both did when we were in a similar state of mind at summit meetings. We

24

would sense that we were either too tired or too angry—or both—to be able to think straight, and we would go to bed."

Sunday clasped Henry's hand. "That's exactly my point. Suppose Tommy actually staggered upstairs under his own steam, leaving Arabella behind. And suppose someone else really *had* followed her there, someone who knew what she was doing that evening. We have to find out who Arabella might have been with earlier. And we should talk to Tommy's housekeeper. She left shortly after Arabella arrived. Maybe there was a car parked on the steet that she noticed. And the countess from Palm Beach who called, who so urgently wanted to talk to Tommy. We've got to contact *her;* it's probably nothing, but you never know what she might be able to tell us."

"Agreed," Henry said admiringly. "As usual, we're on the same wavelength, only you're farther along than I am. I actually hadn't given any thought to talking to the countess." He reached his arm around Sunday and pulled her closer. "Come here. Do you realize that I have not kissed you since 11:10 this morning?" he asked softly.

Sunday caressed his lips with the tip of her index finger. "Ah, then it's more than my steel-trap mind that appeals to you?"

"You've noticed." Henry kissed her fingertip, then grasped her hand and lowered it, removing any obstruction between his lips and hers.

Sunday pulled back. "Just one more thing, Henry. You've got to make sure that Tommy doesn't agree to a plea bargain before we at least try to help him."

"And how am I supposed to do that?" he asked.

"An executive order, of course."

"Darling, I'm no longer president."

"Ah, but in Tommy's eyes you are."

"All right, I'll try. But here's another executive order: stop talking."

In the front seat, the Secret Service agents glanced in the rearview mirror, then grinned at each other.

Henry was up by sunrise the next morning for a ride around a portion of the two-thousand-acre property with the estate manager. Back by 8:30, he was joined by Sunday in the breakfast room, which overlooked the classic English garden at the back of the house. The room itself was decorated to complement the view, with a wealth of botanical prints set against the background of Belgian linen awning-stripe wall covering. It gave the room a feeling of being constantly filled with flowers, and as Sunday frequently observed, was a long way from the upstairs apartment in the two-family house in Jersey City where she had been raised, and where her parents still lived.

"Don't forget that Congress goes into session next week," Sunday said as she eased into her second cup of coffee. "Whatever I can do to help Tommy, I have to start working on it right now. My suggestion would be that I begin by finding out everything I can about Arabella. Did Marvin finish the complete background check we asked for?"

The Marvin she referred to was Marvin Klein, the man who ran Henry's office, which was situated in the estate's former carriage house. Possessed of a droll sense of humor, Marvin called himself the chief of staff for a government in exile, referring to the fact that following Henry Britland's second term, there had been a groundswell of opinion urging a change in the restriction that a United States president could serve only two terms. A poll at the time showed that eighty percent of the electorate wanted that prohibition amended to read no more than two *consecutive* terms. Quite obviously, a majority of the American public wanted Henry Parker Britland IV back in residence at 1600 Pennsylvania Avenue.

"I've got it right here," Henry said. "I just read it. It would appear that the late Arabella successfully managed to bury quite a bit of her background. Some of the juicy bits that Marvin's sources were able to come up with include the fact that she had a previous marriage which ended in a divorce that saw her taking her ex to the cleaners, and that her longtime on-again, off-again boyfriend, Alfred Barker, spent some time in prison for bribing athletes."

"Really! Is he out of prison now?"

"Not only is he out, my dear, but he had dinner with Arabella the night she died."

Sunday's jaw dropped. "Darling, how on earth did Marvin ever discover that?"

"How does Marvin ever discover anything? All I know is that he has his sources. And furthermore, it seems that Alfred Barker lives in Yonkers, which as you probably know is not far from Tarrytown. Her ex-husband is said to be happily remarried and does not live in the area."

"Marvin learned all this overnight?" Sunday asked, her eyes bright with excitement.

Henry nodded in answer, as Sims, the butler, refilled his coffee cup. "Thank you, Sims. And not only that," he continued, "he also learned that apparently Alfred Barker was still very fond of Arabella, however improbable that may sound, and had recently been heard bragging to friends that now that she had ditched the old guy, she'd be getting back together with him."

"What does Barker do now?" Sunday asked.

"Well, technically he owns a plumbing supply store, but Marvin's sources say that actually it is a front for a numbers racket, which he apparently runs pretty much on his own. My favorite bit of information, though, is that our Mr. Barker is known to have a violent temper when double-crossed."

Sunday scrunched her face as though deep in thought. "Hmmm. Let's see now. He had dinner with Arabella just before she barged in on Tommy. He hates being double-crossed, which probably means he is also very jealous, and he has a terrible temper." She looked at her husband. "Are you thinking what I'm thinking?"

"Exactly."

"I *knew* this was a crime of passion!" Sunday said excitedly. "Only it appears that the passion was not on Tommy's part. Okay, so I'll go see Barker today, as well as Tommy's housekeeper. What was her name?"

"Dora, I believe," Henry replied. Then he corrected himself: "No, no—that was the housekeeper who worked for them for years. Great old lady. I believe Tommy said that she retired shortly after Constance died. No, if memory serves me, the one he has now, and that we caught a glimpse of yesterday, is named Lillian West."

"That's right. The woman with the braids and the Lexus," Sunday said. "So I'll take on Barker and the housekeeper. What are you going to do?"

"I'm flying down to Palm Beach to meet with this Countess Condazzi, but I'll be home for dinner. And you, my dear, have to promise me that you'll be careful. Remember that this Alfred Barker is clearly an unsavory character. I don't want you giving the Secret Service guys the slip."

"Okay."

"I mean it, Sunday," Henry said in the quiet, serious tone he had used so effectively to make his cabinet members quake in their boots.

"Oooh, you're one tough hombre," Sunday said smiling. "Okay, I promise. I'll stick to them like glue. And you fly safely." She kissed the top of his head and then left the breakfast room, humming "Hail to the Chief."

Some four hours later, having piloted his jet to the West Palm Beach airport, Henry arrived at the Spanish-style mansion that was the home of Countess Condazzi. "Wait outside," he instructed his Secret Service detail.

The countess appeared to be in her mid-sixties, a small, slender woman with exquisite features and calm gray eyes. She greeted Henry with cordial warmth, then got straight to the point. "I was so glad to get your call, Mr. President," she said. "I read the news accounts of Tommy's terrible situation, and I have been so anxious to talk to him. I know how much he must be suffering, but he won't return my phone calls. Look, I *know* Tommy could not have committed this crime. We've been friends since we were children; we went to school together, including college, and in all that time there was never a moment when he so lost control of himself. Even when others around him were being fresh or disorderly, as they tended to be at the prom, and even when he was drinking, Tommy was always a gentleman. He took care of me, and when the prom was over, he took me home. No, Tommy simply could not have done this thing."

"That's exactly the way I see it," Henry said in agreement. "So you grew up with him?"

"Across the street from each other in Rye. We dated all through college, but then he met Constance and I met Eduardo Condazzi, who was from Spain. I got married, and a year later, when Eduardo's older brother died and he inherited the title and the family's vineyards, we moved to Spain. Eduardo passed away three years ago. My son is now the count and lives in Spain still, but I thought it was time for me to come home. Then, after all these years, I bumped into Tommy when he was visiting friends down here for a golfing weekend. It was so wonderful to see him again. The years just seemed to melt away."

And love was rekindled, Henry thought. "Countess . . ."

"Betsy," she instructed firmly.

"All right, Betsy, I have to be blunt. Did you and Tommy begin to pick up where you left off years ago?"

"Well, yes and no," Betsy said slowly. "I made it clear to him how very glad I was to see him again, and I think he felt the same way about me. But you see, I also think that Tommy never really gave himself a chance to grieve for Constance. In fact, we talked about it at length. It was obvious to me that his involvement with Arabella Young was his way of trying to escape the grieving process. I advised him to drop Arabella, and then to give himself a period of mourning, something like six months to a year. But then, I told him, he had to call me and take me to a prom."

Henry studied Betsy Condazzi's face, her wistful smile, her eyes filled with memories. "Did he agree?" he asked.

"Not completely. He said that he was selling his house and was going to move down here permanently." She smiled. "He said that he'd be ready long before six months were up, to take me to the prom."

Henry paused before asking the next question: "If Arabella Young had gone to the tabloids with a story claiming that during my administration and even before his wife's death, Tommy and I had thrown wild, debauched parties in the White House, what would your reaction be?"

"Why, I'd know it wasn't true," she said simply. "And Tommy knows me well enough to be sure that he could count on my support."

On the return flight to Newark airport, Henry let his pilot take over the controls. His time was spent deep in thought. It was becoming increasingly clear to him that Tommy was being set up. Obviously he was aware that his future had promised a second chance at happiness and that he didn't have to kill in order to safeguard that chance. No, it just didn't make sense that he would have killed Arabella Young. But how were they going to prove it? He wondered if Sunday was having any better luck in finding a likely motive for Arabella's murder.

Alfred Barker was not a man who inspired instinctive liking, Sunday thought as she sat across from him in the office of his plumbing supply store.

He appeared to be in his mid-forties, a thick, barrel-chested man with heavily lidded eyes, a sallow complexion, and salt-and-pepper hair, which he combed dramatically across his skull in an obvious effort to hide a growing bald spot. His open shirt, however, revealed a wealth of hair on his chest. The only other distinctive thing she noticed about him was a jagged scar on the back of his right hand.

Sunday felt a fleeting moment of gratitude as she thought of Henry's lean, muscular body, his altogether pleasing appearance, including his famous "stubborn" jaw and the sable brown eyes that could convey or, if necessary, conceal emotion. And while she frequently chaffed at the omnipresent Secret Service men—after all, she had never been a First Lady, so why should she need them now?—at this moment, closeted in this squalid room with this hostile man, she was glad to know that they stood just outside the partially open door.

She had introduced herself as Sandra O'Brien, and it was obvious that Alfred Barker did not have a clue that the rest of her name was Britland.

"So why do you wanna talk to me about Arabella?" Barker asked as he lit a cigar.

"I want to start by saying that I'm very sorry about her death," Sunday said sincerely. "I understand that you and she were very close. But, you see, I know Mr. Shipman." She paused, then explained, "My husband at one time worked with him. And there seems to be a conflicting version of who broke up his relationship with Ms. Young."

"What does that matter? Arabella was sick of the old creep," Barker said. "Arabella always liked me."

"But she got engaged to Thomas Shipman," Sunday protested.

"Yeah, but I knew that would never last. All he had was a fat wallet. You see, Arabella got married when she was

32

eighteen to some jerk who was so dumb he needed to be introduced to himself every morning. But Arabella was smart. The guy may have been stupid, but he was worth hanging onto 'cause there were big bucks in the family. So she hung around for three or four years, let him pay for her to go to college, get her teeth fixed, whatever, then waited until his very rich uncle died, got him to commingle the money, and then dumped him. She cleaned up in the divorce."

Alfred Barker relit the tip of his cigar and exhaled noisily, then leaned back in his chair. "What a shrewd cookie she was. A natural."

"And was it then that she started seeing you?" Sunday prodded.

"Right. But then I had a little misunderstanding with the government and ended up in the can for a spell. She got herself a job with a fancy public relations firm, and when a chance to move to their Washington branch came up a couple of years ago, she grabbed it."

Barker inhaled deeply on the cigar, then coughed noisily. "Nope, you couldn't hold Arabella down, not that I ever wanted to. When I got sprung last year, she used to call me all the time and tell me about that jerk, Shipman, but it was a good setup for her, because he was always giving her jewelry, and she was always meeting fancy people." Barker leaned across the desk and said meaningfully, "Including the president of the United States, Henry Parker Britland the Fourth."

He paused, once again leaning back in his chair. He looked at Sunday accusingly. "How many people in this country ever sat down at the table and traded jokes with the president of the United States? Have you?" he challenged.

"No, not with the president," Sunday said honestly, remembering that first night at the White House when she had declined Henry's invitation to dinner.

"See what I mean?" Barker crowed triumphantly.

"Well, obviously, as secretary of state, Thomas Shipman was able to provide great contacts for Arabella. But according to Mr. Shipman, *he* was the one who was breaking off the relationship. *Not* Arabella."

"Yeah. Well, so what?"

"Then why would he kill her?"

Barker's face darkened, and he slammed his fist on the desk. "I warned Arabella not to threaten him with that tabloid routine. I told her that this time she was running with a different crowd. But it had worked for her before, so she wouldn't listen to me."

"She got away with it before!" Sunday exclaimed, remembering that this was exactly the scenario she had suggested to Henry. "Who else did she try to blackmail?"

"Oh, some guy she worked with. I don't know his name. Some small potatoes. But it's never a good idea to mess around with a guy who's got the kind of clout Shipman has. Remember what he did to Castro?"

"How much did she talk about her efforts to blackmail him?"

"Not much, and then only to me. I kept telling her not to try it, but she figured it would be worth a couple of bucks." Unlikely tears welled in Alfred Barker's eyes. "I really liked her. But she was so stubborn. She just wouldn't listen." He paused, apparently lost for a moment in reflection. "I warned her. There was even this quotation that I showed her."

Sunday's head jerked back in involuntary reaction to Barker's startling statement.

"I like quotations," he said. "I read them for laughs and for insight, or whatever, if you know what I mean."

Sunday nodded her head. "My husband is very fond of quotations. He says they contain wisdom."

"Yeah, that's what I mean! What's your husband do?"

"He's unemployed at the moment," Sunday replied, looking down at her hands.

"That's tough. Does he know anything about plumbing?"

"Not much."

"Do you think he could run numbers?"

Sunday shook her head sadly. "No, mostly he just stays home. And he reads a lot, like the quotations you were mentioning," she said, trying to get the conversation back on track.

"Yeah, the one I read Arabella fit her so well it was amazing. She had a big mouth. A real big mouth. I came across this quote and showed it to her. I always told her that her big mouth would get her in trouble, and boy it did."

Barker rummaged through the top drawer of his desk, then pulled out a tattered piece of paper. "Here it is. Read this." He thrust a page at Sunday that obviously had been torn from a book of quotations. One entry on the page was circled in red:

> Beyond this stone, a lump of clay,
> Lies Arabella Young,
> Who on the 24th of May
> Began to hold her tongue.

"It comes from an old English tombstone. Just like that! Except for the date, is that a coincidence or is that a coincidence?" Barker sighed heavily and then slumped back in his chair. "Yeah, I'm sure gonna miss Arabella. She was fun."

"You had dinner with her the night she died, didn't you?"

"Yeah."

"Did you drop her off at the Shipman house?"

"Nah. I told her she should give it a rest, but she wouldn't listen. So I put her in a cab. She was planning to borrow his car to get home." Barker shook his head. "Only she wasn't planning to return it. She was sure he'd give her anything just to keep her from talking to the tabloids." He fell silent for a moment. "Instead, look what he did to her."

Barker stood up, his face twisted with fresh anger. "I hope they fry him!"

Sunday got to her feet. "The death penalty in New York State is administered by lethal injection, but I get your drift. Tell me, Mr. Barker, what did you do after you put Arabella in a cab?"

"You know, I've been expecting to be asked that, but the cops didn't even bother talking to me. They knew they got Arabella's killer from the start. So, after I put her in the cab, I went to my mother's and took her to the movies. I do that once a month. I was at her house by quarter of nine, and in line to buy tickets at two minutes of nine. The ticket guy knows me. The kid who sells popcorn at the theater knows me. The woman who was sitting next to me is Mama's friend, and she knows I was there for the whole show. So I didn't murder Arabella, but I know who did!"

Barker pounded his fist on the desk, sending an empty soda bottle crashing to the floor. "You wanna help Shipman? Decorate his cell."

Sunday's Secret Service guards were suddenly beside her, staring intently at Barker. "I wouldn't pound the desk in this lady's presence," one of them suggested icily.

For the first time since she had entered the office, Sunday noticed, Alfred Barker was at a loss for words.

Thomas Acker Shipman had not been pleased to receive the call from Marvin Klein, Henry Britland's aide, informing him of the president's request that he delay the plea-bargaining process. What is the use? Shipman wondered, disgruntled by not being able to get on with it. It was inevitable that he would have to go to jail, and he just wanted to get it over with. Besides, this house already had taken on the aspects of a prison. Once the plea-bargaining was finished, the media would have a surge of interest in him, but then he would be dropped and they would be on to another poor slob. A sixty-five-year-old man going to prison for ten or fifteen years didn't remain hot copy for long.

The only thing that keeps them churning so much, he thought as he once again peered out at the mass of reporters still camped outside his house, is the speculation about whether or not I'll go to trial. Once that's been resolved, and it's clear that I'm taking my medicine without putting up a fight, they'll lose interest.

His housekeeper, Lillian West, had arrived promptly at eight o'clock that morning. He had hoped to discourage her coming today by putting on the safety chain, but apparently all he succeeded in doing was in making her more determined than ever to get in. When her key did not gain her entrance, she had pushed the doorbell firmly and called his name until he let her in. "You need taking care of, whether you think so or not," she had said, sharply brushing aside the objection he had voiced yesterday, that he didn't want her private life invaded by the media, and that, in fact, he really did prefer to be left alone.

And so she had gone about her usual daily chores, cleaning rooms that he would never again get to live in, and fixing meals for which he had no appetite. Shipman watched her as she moved about the house. Lillian was a handsome woman, an excellent housekeeper, and a *cordon bleu* cook, but her overly bossy tendencies occasionally made him wistfully remember Dora, the housekeeper who had been with him and Connie for some twenty years. So what if she had sometimes burned the bacon, she had always been a pleasant fixture in their home.

Also, Dora had been of the old school, while Lillian clearly believed in the equality of the employee to the employer. Nevertheless, Shipman realized that for the short time he would be in the house before going to prison, he could manage to put up with Lillian's takeover attitude. He would just make the best of it by trying to enjoy the creature comforts of delicious meals and properly served wine.

Recognizing that he could not cut himself off completely from the outside world, and acknowledging that he actually needed to be available to his lawyer, Shipman had turned on the telephone answering machine and had begun taking calls, although screening out those that weren't necessary. When he heard Sunday's voice, however, he gladly picked up the phone.

"Tommy, I'm in the car and on my way to your house from Yonkers," Sunday explained. "I want to talk to your housekeeper. Is she in today, and if not, do you know where I can reach her?"

"Lillian is here."

"Wonderful. Don't let her leave until I have had a chance to visit with her. I should be there in about an hour."

"I can't imagine what she'll be able to tell you that the police haven't already heard."

"Tommy, I've just talked with Arabella's boyfriend. He knew of her plan to extort money from you, and from what he said, I gather that it was a stunt that she had pulled on at least one other person. We've got to find out who that person was. It's entirely possible that someone followed Arabella to your house that night, and we hope that when Lillian left she might have seen something—a car, maybe —that didn't seem significant at the time but could prove to be important. The police never really investigated any other possible suspects, and since Henry and I are convinced that you didn't do it, we're going to sniff around for them. So buck up! It ain't over till it's over."

Shipman hung up and turned to see Lillian West standing in the doorway to his study. Obviously she had been listening to his conversation. Even so, he smiled pleasantly. "Mrs. Britland is on her way here to talk to you," he said. "She and the president seem to feel that I may not be guilty of killing Arabella after all and are doing some sleuthing on their own. They have a theory that might prove to be very helpful to me, and that's what she wants to speak to you about."

"That's wonderful," Lillian West said, her voice flat and her tone chilly. "I can't wait to talk to her."

Sunday's next call was to Henry, on his plane. They exchanged reports on what they had learned so far, he from the countess and she from Alfred Barker. After Sunday's revelation about Arabella's habit of blackmailing the men she dated, she added a cautionary note: "The only problem with all this is that no matter who else might have wanted to kill Arabella, proving that that person walked into Tommy's house undetected, loaded the gun that happened to be lying there, and then pulled the trigger is going to be difficult."

"Difficult maybe, but not impossible," Henry said by way of reassurance. "I'll get Marvin started right away on checking out Arabella's last places of employment, and maybe he can find out who she might have been involved with there."

After saying good-bye to Sunday, Henry sat back to ponder what he had just learned about Arabella's past. He felt a strong sense of unease, but he couldn't quite put it together. He had a growing premonition that something was wrong, but he couldn't put his finger on just what it was.

He leaned back in the swivel chair that was his favorite spot on the plane, other than the flight deck. It was something Sunday had said, he decided, but what was it? With almost total recall, he reviewed their conversation. Of course, he said to himself when he reached that point in his recollection, it was Sunday's observation about the difficulty in trying to prove that some unknown person had walked into Tommy's house, loaded the pistol, and pulled the trigger.

That was it! It didn't have to be an outsider. There was one person who *could* have done that, who knew that Tommy felt both sick and overwhelmingly tired, who knew that Arabella was there, who in fact had let her *in*. *The housekeeper!*

She was relatively new. Chances are that Tommy hadn't really had her checked out, probably didn't know much of anything about her.

Quickly, Henry phoned Countess Condazzi. Let her still be home, he prayed silently. When her now-familiar voice answered, he wasted no time in getting to the point of his call: "Betsy, did Tommy ever say anything to you about his new housekeeper?"

She hesitated before answering. "Well, yes, but only jokingly."

"What do you mean?"

"Oh, you know how it is," she responded. "There are so many women in their fifties and sixties who are unattached, but there are so few men. When I spoke to Tommy last—it was the morning of the day that poor girl was killed—I said I had a dozen friends who are widowed or divorced who would be jealous because of his interest in me, and that if he showed up down here, he would be the center of attention. I remember that he said that except for me, he intended to steer clear of unattached women, and that, in fact, he had just had a most unpleasant experience in this regard." She paused before continuing. "It seems that only that morning he had told his new housekeeper that he was putting his house on the market and would be moving to Palm Beach. He confided to her that he was finished with Arabella because someone else had become important to him. Later, when he was thinking back over the conversation and her reaction to it, he realized that the housekeeper may have gotten the crazy idea that he had meant *her.* So he made a special point of informing her that, of course, he would not need her services once the house was sold and, naturally, would not be taking her with him to Florida. He recounted that she at first had seemed shocked and then had become cool and distant." Again the countess paused, then gasped, "Goodness, you don't think she could have had anything to do with this mess Tommy's in, do you?"

"I'm afraid I'm beginning to, Betsy," Henry replied. "Look, I'll get back to you. I've got to get my man on this right away." He broke the connection and swiftly dialed Marvin Klein. "Marvin," he said. "I've got a hunch about Secretary Shipman's housekeeper, Lillian West. Do a complete check on her. Immediately."

Marvin Klein did not like to break the law as he would be doing by penetrating private computer records, but he knew that when his boss said "Immediately," the matter had to be urgent.

It was only a matter of minutes before he had assembled a dossier on fifty-six-year-old Lillian West, including her rather extensive record of traffic violations and, more to the point, her employment history. Marvin frowned as he began to read. West was a college graduate, had an M.A., and had taught home economics at a number of colleges, the last one being Wren College in New Hampshire. Then, six years ago, she had left there and taken a job as a housekeeper.

Since then she had held four different positions. Her references—citing her punctuality, her high standard of work, and her cooking ability—were good but not enthusiastic. Marvin decided to check on them himself.

Less than a half hour after Henry's call, Marvin was on the phone to the former president, who was still winging his way back from Florida. "Sir, the records indicate that Lillian West, while employed in various college-level teaching positions, had a history of troubled relationships with her superiors. Six years ago she left her last teaching job and went to work as a housekeeper for a widower in Vermont. He died ten months later, apparently of a heart attack. She then went to work for a divorced executive, who unfortunately died within the year. Before she went to work for Secretary Shipman, her employer was an eighty-year-old millionaire; he fired her but gave her a good reference nonetheless. I spoke to him. He said that while Ms. West was an excellent housekeeper and cook, she also was quite presumptuous and seemed to put no stock in the more traditional relationship between the head of the house and the housekeeper. In fact, he said that it was when he became aware that she had set her mind on marrying him that he decided she would have to go, and shortly after that he showed her the door."

"Did this man report ever having any health problems?" Henry asked quietly as he absorbed the possibilities that were presented by Lillian West's troubled history.

"I did think to ask him that, sir. He said that he is in robust health now, but that during the last several weeks of Ms. West's employment, specifically after he had given her notice, he experienced extreme fatigue, followed by an undiagnosed illness that culminated in pneumonia."

Tommy had spoken of a heavy cold and overwhelming

fatigue. Henry's hand gripped the phone. "Good job, Marvin. Thanks."

"Sir, I'm afraid there's more. According to the records, Ms. West's hobby is hunting, and apparently she is very familiar with guns. Finally, I spoke to the president of Wren College, where she had her last teaching job. As he remembered it, Ms. West was forced to resign. He said that she had displayed symptoms of being deeply disturbed but refused all attempts at counseling."

Henry ended the conversation with his aide as a wave of anxiety swept over him. Sunday was on her way right now to see Lillian West, totally unaware of any of the background Marvin had uncovered. She would unwittingly alert the housekeeper to the fact that they were looking into the very strong possibility that someone other than Thomas Shipman had murdered Arabella Young. There was no telling how the woman might react. Henry's hand had never shaken even at summit meetings, but right now his fingers could barely punch the numbers to reach Sunday's car phone.

Secret Service agent Art Dowling answered. "We're at Secretary Shipman's place now, sir. Mrs. Britland is inside."

"Get her," Henry snapped. "Tell her I *must* speak to her."

"Right away, sir."

Several minutes passed before Agent Dowling was back on the phone. "Sir, there may be a problem. We've rung the doorbell repeatedly, but no one is answering."

Sunday and Tommy sat side by side on the leather couch in the library, staring into the muzzle of a revolver. Opposite them, Lillian West sat erect and steady as she held the gun. The persistent pealing of the front doorbell did not seem to distract her.

"Your palace guard, no doubt," she said sarcastically.

The woman is crazy, Sunday thought as she stared into the housekeeper's wild eyes. She's crazy and she's desperate. She knows she has nothing to lose by killing us, and she is just nuts enough to do it.

Sunday thought next of the Secret Service agents waiting outside. Art Dowling and Clint Carr were with her today. What would they do when no one answered the door? They'd probably force their way in, she reasoned. And when they do, she will shoot Tommy and me, she thought, her level of alarm increasing. I know she will.

"You have everything," Lillian West said to Sunday, her eyes fixed on her prisoner, her voice low and angry. "You're beautiful, you're young, you've got an important job, and you're married to a rich and attractive man. Well, I just hope that you have enjoyed the time you've had with him."

"Yes, I have," Sunday said calmly. "He is a wonderful man and husband, and I want more time with him."

"Too bad, but that's not going to happen, and it's your fault. This wouldn't be necessary if you'd just let well enough alone. What difference would it make if he"— Lillian West paused, her eyes cutting momentarily to Tommy—"if he went to prison? He's not worth your trouble. He's no good. He tricked me. He lied to me. He promised to take me to Florida. He was going to marry me." She paused again, this time turning her full glare on the former secretary of state. "Of course, he wasn't as rich as the others, but he has enough to get by. I've gone through all his papers here and I know." A smile played on her lips. "And he's nicer than the others, too. I liked that especially. We could have been very happy."

"Lillian, I didn't lie to you," Tommy said quietly. "Think back over all that I ever said to you, and I think you'll agree. I do like you though, and I think you need help. I want to see that you get it. I promise that both Sunday and I will do everything we can for you."

"What, by getting me another housekeeping job?" Lillian snapped. "Cleaning, cooking, shopping. No thanks! I traded teaching silly girls for this kind of drudgery because I thought that somebody would finally appreciate me, would want to take care of me. But it didn't happen. After I waited on all of them, they still treated me like dirt." She directed her gaze again at Tommy. "I thought you were going to be different, but you're not. You're just like all the rest."

While they had been talking, the pealing of the doorbell had stopped. Sunday knew that the Secret Service men would be looking for some way to get in, and she had no doubt that they would succeed. Then she froze. When Lillian West had admitted her, she had reset the alarm. "We don't want one of those reporters trying to sneak in," she had explained.

If Art or Clint tries to open a window, the alarm will go off, Sunday thought, and once that happens, Tommy and I are goners. She felt Tommy's hand brush hers. He's thinking the same thing, she realized. My God, what can we do? She had often heard the expression "staring death in the face," but it wasn't until this moment that she knew what it meant. *Henry,* she thought, *Henry! Please don't let this woman take away our life together.*

Tommy's hand was closed over hers now. His index finger was insistently jabbing the back of her hand. He was trying to send her a signal. But what? she wondered. What did he want her to do?

Henry stayed on the line, anxious not to break the connection to the Secret Service agent outside Tommy Shipman's house. Agent Dowling was on his cellular phone now, and continued to talk to the former president as he carefully worked his way around the house. "Sir, all the draperies are drawn, in virtually every room. We've contacted the local police and they should be here any moment. Clint is at the back of the house, climbing a tree that has branches that reach near some windows. We might be able to get in undetected through there. The problem is that we have no way of knowing where they are within the house."

My God, Henry thought. It would take at least an hour to get the special equipment over there that would enable us to follow their movement inside the house. I'm just afraid we don't have that time to spare. Sunday's face loomed in his mind. *Sunday! Sunday!* She *had* to be all right. He wanted to get out and push the plane to make it go faster. He wanted to order the army out. He wanted to *be* there. *Now!* He shook his head. He had never felt so helpless. Then he heard Dowling swear furiously.

"What is it, Art?" he shouted. "What is it?"

"Sir, the draperies in the right front downstairs room just opened, and I am sure I heard shots being fired inside."

* * *

47

"That stupid woman provided me with the perfect opportunity," Lillian West was saying. "I knew I was running out of time, that I wouldn't be able to kill you slowly, the way I wanted. But this was just as good, really. This way I not only punished you but that dreadful woman as well."

"Then you *did* kill Arabella?" Tommy exclaimed.

"Of course I did," she snapped impatiently. "It was so easy, too. You see, I didn't leave that evening. I showed her to this room, woke you up, said good night, shut the door, and hid in the coat closet. I heard it all. And I knew the pistol was there, ready for use. When you staggered upstairs, I knew it would be only a matter of minutes before you lost consciousness." She paused and smiled mischievously. "My sleeping pills are much more effective than the ones you were used to, aren't they? They have special ingredients." She smiled again. "And a few interesting viruses as well. Why do you think your cold has improved so much since that night? Because you haven't let me in to give you your pills. If you had, your cold would be pneumonia by now."

"You were *poisoning* Tommy?" Sunday exclaimed.

Lillian West stared indignantly at the younger woman. "I was *punishing* him," she said firmly. Then she turned again to Shipman. "Once you were safely upstairs, I went back into the library. Arabella was rummaging around on your desk and was flustered at first by having me catch her. She said she was looking for your car keys, said that you weren't feeling well and had told her to drive herself home, that she would be back with the car in the morning. Then she asked me what I was doing back there, since I had told you both good night. I said I had come back because I had promised to turn your old pistol in at the police station but had forgotten to take it. The poor fool stood there and watched me while I picked it up and loaded it. Her last words were, 'Isn't it dangerous to load it? I'm sure Mr. Shipman didn't intend that.' "

Lillian West began to laugh, a high-pitched, almost hysterical cackle. Tears ran from her eyes and her body shook, but through it all she kept the gun trained on them.

She's working up to killing us, Sunday thought, for the first moment fully realizing that there was little hope for escape. Tommy's finger was still jabbing the back of her hand.

" *'Isn't it dangerous to load it?'* " West repeated, mimicking Arabella's last words, her own voice cracking with loud, raucous laughter. " *'I'm sure Mr. Shipman didn't intend that!'* "

She rested her gun hand on her left arm, steadying it. The laughter ended.

"Would you consider opening the draperies?" Shipman asked. "At least let me see sunlight one more time."

Lillian West's smile was mirthless. "Why bother with that? You're about to see the shining light at the end of the tunnel," she told him.

The draperies, Sunday thought suddenly. That was what Tommy had been trying to get across to her. Yesterday when he had lowered the shade in the kitchen he'd mentioned that the electronic device that worked the draperies in this room was defective, that it sounded a lot like a gunshot when it was used. Sunday looked around carefully. The control for the drapes was lying on the armrest of the couch. She had to get to it. It was their only hope.

Sunday pressed Tommy's hand by way of indicating that she finally understood. Then, as a prayer raced through her mind, she reached out and with a lightning-fast movement pressed the button that would open the drapes.

The sound, loud as a gunshot, just as promised, made Lillian West whirl her head around. In that instant, both Tommy and Sunday leapt from the couch. Tommy threw himself at the woman's lower body, but it was Sunday who slammed West's hand upward just as she began to pull the gun's trigger. As they struggled, several shots were fired. Sunday felt a burning sensation in her left arm, but it did not deter her. Unable to wrest the gun from the woman, she threw herself on top of her and kicked at the chair so that it toppled over with all three of them on it, just as the shattering of glass signaled the welcome arrival of her Secret Service detail.

Ten minutes later, a handkerchief wrapped securely over the superficial wound on her arm, Sunday was on the phone to a totally unnerved ex-president of the United States.

"I'm fine," she said for the fifteenth time, "just fine. And Tommy is fine, too. Lillian West is in a straitjacket and on her way out of here. So stop worrying. Everything has been taken care of."

"But you could have been killed," Henry said, not for the first time. He didn't want to break the phone connection. He didn't want to let his wife stop talking. This had been too close. He couldn't bear the thought that he might ever *not* be able to hear her voice.

"But I *wasn't* killed," Sunday said briskly. "And, Henry, we were both right. It was definitely a crime of passion. It was just that we were a little slow in figuring out *whose* passion was the cause of the crime."

They All Ran
After the
President's
Wife

◆

"It's the Oval Office calling, Mr. President."

Henry Parker Britland IV sighed. "Do not go gentle into that good night," he thought. Marvin Klein, his longtime right-hand associate, still seemed incapable of calling his successor, the current president of the United States, anything other than "the Oval Office."

The call came as Henry was seated at his desk in the library of Drumdoe, his New Jersey country home. The late afternoon winter sun was filtering through the tall leaded-pane windows and shimmered over the satiny paneling of the magnificent Gothic Revival decor. He'd set out to work on his memoirs but realized with a start that he had been daydreaming. Sunday, his bride of less than a year, and a member of Congress, was in Washington, and Henry had found himself wishing away the next three days until she would be here with him again.

As always, his thoughts of her were filled with longing. Sunday—surely no one person could really be that beautiful, that intelligent, that witty, that compassionate. There were times when he truly felt that he must have dreamt her into existence. His Sunday: the slender, blond congresswoman, who on an impulse he had chosen to flirt with at his last reception in the White House, just before leaving office after his second term. With an unconscious smile, he recalled her calm, reproachful response.

"Ahem. The Oval Office, Mr. President," Klein insisted, effectively breaking his reverie.

Henry picked up the phone. "Mr. President," he said warmly.

He could envision Desmond Ogilvey—Des, as he was known to friends—seated at his desk, scholarly in his appearance, with his shock of white hair, his long, lean frame erect, his sober dark blue suit and tie.

He knew his former vice president had never forgotten the fact that nine years ago Henry had plucked him from the relative obscurity of being a congressman from Wyoming by choosing him to be his running mate. It was a decision challenged initially by the media, many of whom called it a gamble.

"To you it may be a gamble," Henry had replied, "but to me, this is a man who has served in Congress for ten terms, who has been quietly responsible for some of the most effective legislation passed by the last ten Congresses. It is my firm conviction that if I am elected by the voters, and if anything were to happen to me during my time in office, then I will go to my Maker knowing that the country I love is in the worthiest hands I could have found for it."

Realizing that the silence that followed his greeting was stretching out unusually long, Henry spoke again: "Des?"

"Mr. President," Desmond Ogilvey replied, but there was none of the usual jocularity in his tone.

Henry instantly realized that this was not a social call, and cut immediately to the chase. "What's wrong, Des?"

Again a pause. Then, "It's Sunday. Henry, I'm sorry."

"Sunday!" Henry's breathing ceased. He felt suddenly that his heart had stopped beating, that his whole body was being suspended, frozen in that moment.

"Henry, I don't know how to tell you this. We have a terrible situation. Sunday is missing. Her Secret Service guys were found unconscious, still in the car. The same thing happened to the follow-up detail. Apparently some kind of anesthetic had been used to knock them out, enough to immobilize everyone in both cars. By the time the agents came to, Sunday was gone."

"Any apparent motive?" Henry was breathing again, willing himself into calmness. He was aware that his voice was even, that Marvin was staring at him, that he was pressing the buzzer to signal the Secret Service detail waiting outside.

"We think so. A phone call was placed to the switchboard at the Treasury. The caller claimed to have Sunday, or at least to know of her whereabouts. You can tell us if the call is authentic. Does Sunday have a nasty bruise on her upper right arm, just below the shoulder?"

Henry nodded, then whispered, "Yes."

"So that means that the call must be legitimate. Apparently she hadn't mentioned the bruise to anyone on her staff, because they claim to know nothing of it."

"She was thrown from her horse while we were riding last Saturday," Henry said, remembering the momentary fright he had experienced then, contrasting it to the almost paralyzing sense of foreboding he felt now. He became aware that the five Secret Service men currently on duty were standing in an arc around the desk. He nodded to Jack Collins, the senior agent, indicating that he should pick up the phone extension on the table next to the deep red Moroccan leather sofa.

"Collins is on, Des," Henry said. "Sunday is just learning to ride. When she got the bruise, she joked that if she told anybody about it, the tabloids would start calling me a wife beater." He realized with a start that he was rambling. He had to get himself to focus. "Des, how much money do they want? I'll get it ready now, no questions."

"I wish it were money, Henry. Unfortunately they have announced to us that unless we release Claudus Jovunet by tomorrow night, we can start dragging the Atlantic for Sunday's body."

Claudus Jovunet. It was a name Henry Britland knew well. A particularly heartless terrorist; a former mercenary; a paid assassin. His most recent known crime, and the one that finally led to his capture, had been the successful bombing of a company jet of Uranus Oil, a tragedy that had claimed the lives of the company's twenty-two top executives. After a career that spanned fifteen years of terror, Jovunet had finally been brought to justice and was now serving consecutive life sentences in the federal prison at Marion, Ohio. While Henry had played no real part in getting the killer into prison, he had taken a particular satisfaction that it had happened during his term of office.

"What are the terms of exchange?" Henry asked, knowing as the question left his lips that Des might not feel that he could allow the government to be held up by a terrorist organization.

"The instructions are to put Jovunet on the new supersonic transport. As you are aware, it is currently on display at National here in Washington, preparatory to its inaugural flight. They stipulate that there can be only the two pilots on board. The only other instruction is a little on the odd side: they say we should fully stock the galley, but— I'm quoting, now—we can 'skip the caviar.' " The president paused. "They give—and again I am quoting—their 'sacred word' that after the flight lands, the pilots will be permitted to radio the details of where Sunday can be found, quoting again, 'alive and well.' "

"Their 'sacred word,' " Henry snapped bitterly. *Oh, Sunday, Sunday!*

He glanced at Jack Collins who was mouthing the word "weapons."

"What kind of weapons are they demanding, Des?" Henry asked.

"None, oddly enough. If we can believe these people—"

"*Can* we believe these people?" Henry asked, interrupting.

Des sighed. "We have little choice, Henry."

"What are the plans?" Henry held his breath after asking the question, afraid of what he might hear.

"Henry, Jerry is here with me," Des said. Jerry was Jeremy Thomas, secretary of the treasury.

Henry interrupted: "Des, how long can we drag it out while we seem to play along?"

"We're supposed to get another message at one of the Departments at five o'clock. We think we can stall until

Thursday afternoon, at least. Fortunately the *Washington Post* carried a story this morning about several minor mechanical adjustments that have to be made before the new plane can take its first flight on Friday." He paused. "And to put your mind at rest even a little, be assured that we absolutely intend to go through with the exchange."

Henry's body shuddered as he allowed himself the first deep breath in several minutes. He looked at his watch. It was four o'clock Wednesday afternoon. If they were lucky they had twenty-four hours. "I'm on my way, Des," Henry said.

Tom Wyman, the agent second in command, broke the silence that followed the click of the phones: "The helicopter is waiting, sir. The plane is in readiness for immediate departure."

For several long moments Sunday felt so confused and disoriented that she almost had to remind herself of her own name. Where am I? she wondered, as her mind gradually woke up to the realization that something had gone terribly wrong. The immediate physical sensation was of being tied down. Her arms and legs hurt, but there was also a feeling of numbness. Something was holding her body rigid. She twisted slightly, and a mental image came to her of towels and sheets, stiffly flapping in the icy wind on the roof of her grandmother's apartment building in New Jersey. Clothesline, she thought. The harsh, abrasive cords that were confining her felt like old-fashioned clothesline.

Her head still felt groggy and strangely weighted, as though a boulder were pressing down on it. She forced her eyes open but could see nothing. She gasped slightly as she realized that something was covering her face and head, a thick, scratchy cloth of some kind that made her face itchy and warm.

But the rest of her body was cold. Her arms were especially cold. She twisted slightly and realized that she wasn't wearing her jacket. The twisting also made her realize that her right arm was hurting from where the cord was digging into the bruise she had gotten when she fell off Appleby.

Sunday did a quick assessment of her situation: Okay, so I have a piece of burlap or canvas or something over my head, and I am trussed up like a Christmas turkey, she thought. And I am in a cold room somewhere. But where? And what happened? She didn't remember anything. Had there been an accident? Was she in an operating room, confined on the table, waking up in surgery?

Then she remembered: something had happened in the car.

That was it! Something had happened in the car. But what?

She forced herself to try to remember, to calmly go over the events of the day. The House had adjourned at three o'clock. Art and Leo had been waiting for her as they always did, in the area off the cloakroom. She had not gone back to her office as she usually did, because there was a reception at the French embassy that she had to attend and she needed to get home to change for it. So they had gotten in the car and headed across town. Then what?

Sunday tried to force back the moan that she could feel escaping her lips. She'd always prided herself on not being a crybaby. Irrationally she thought back on the time when she was nine years old and had been swinging from a bar in the school yard and had slipped. She had seen the ground rushing up toward her before her forehead had smashed against the pebbled concrete. She hadn't cried then. And she wouldn't cry now. Although then there had been some boys standing around who had seen her fall, so she couldn't cry in front of them, and now she was alone.

No, don't give in, she admonished herself. Think; just think. When had the accident happened? She mentally retraced the steps they had taken. Art had opened the back door of the car for her and waited until she was inside. He'd then slipped in beside Leo, who sat behind the steering wheel. She had waved to Larry and Bill, who were waiting in the follow-up car behind them.

The snow had stopped falling, but the streets were still messy and treacherous. They had passed a couple of fender benders. Despite the hour, it was dark outside, and she had turned on the backseat reading light and had been studying the notes she had taken during the Speaker's speech earlier that day, and then there had been a loud noise, like a muffled explosion. Yes, that was it, an explosion!

And she had looked up. She remembered that they had been passing the Kennedy Center and were almost to Watergate. Art's face. She remembered that he had been looking back at her, then past her, out the back window at the follow-up car. He had shouted, "Step on it, Leo!" But then his voice had faded. Sunday couldn't remember if he had stopped shouting or if it had been she who had stopped hearing, because she remembered feeling weak suddenly.

Yes, she remembered trying to sit up because the car was slowing to a stop. And then the driver's-side door had opened. And that was all she remembered.

It was enough, though, to make her understand that she wasn't in a hospital. Because there hadn't been an accident. No, obviously this had happened on purpose. She had been kidnapped.

But who had done it? And why?

Wherever she was, it was damp and chilly. The cloth over her head was so disorienting. She shook her head, trying to clear it slightly. Whatever the kidnappers had used to knock her out was wearing off, but its residue was leaving her with a powerful headache. What she did know was that she was securely tied down to what felt to be a wooden chair. Was she alone? She couldn't be sure. She sensed that someone was nearby, perhaps even watching her.

She thought suddenly of the Secret Service guys, Art and Leo. Were they there too? If not, what had happened to them? She knew that they would have done anything to protect her. Please, God, don't let them have been murdered, she said in silent prayer.

Henry! She knew he must be frantic. Or does he even know yet that I am missing? How long has it been? For all she knew, it could have been anything from a few minutes to several days since she had been kidnapped. And why has this happened? What benefit can someone get by kidnapping me? If it was money, then she knew that Henry would pay whatever it would take. Somehow, though, she sensed that this wasn't about money at all.

Sunday's throat closed. There was someone there, in the room, with her. She could hear faint breathing, coming closer. Someone was bending over her. Thick, insistent fingers were tracing the contours of her face through the heavy fabric, caressing her neck, reaching up into her hair.

A low, hoarse voice she had to strain to hear whispered, "They're all looking for you. Just like I knew they would. Your husband. The president. The Secret Service. By now they are sniffing all over. But they're like blind mice. Yes, like three blind mice. And they won't find you. At least not until the tide comes in, and by then it won't matter."

Henry did not speak on the flight to Washington. He sat alone in the private compartment of the plane, forcing his mind to focus on what was known about Sunday's kidnapping and on what could be deduced from it. He had to distance himself from the emotional turmoil he felt inwardly and make his mind analyze the situation as he had analyzed dozens of intensely critical situations during his time in the White House. He had to be guided by reason, not simply galvanized by emotion. He had to be like a surgeon, analytical and clearheaded.

But then, in a surge of misery, Henry reminded himself that except in cases of dire emergency, no surgeon would ever operate on his own wife, for fear that his emotions would cloud his judgment.

A scrap of poetry ran through his mind: "These mortal hands because of love have lain like music on your throat. But the music of the soul is delicate, remote . . ." He had no idea of the source of the line but knew that for some reason, at this moment, it was pertinent.

He thought of Sunday, of how easily she fell asleep, while he liked to read, sometimes for hours, after going to bed. Occasionally she would doze off while he was reading to her, or perhaps critiquing out loud something he found especially wrongheaded in one of the many newspapers he read daily.

He remembered that just last Sunday night he had wanted to share something with her but realized that she had fallen asleep. Still, he had brushed her neck with his fingers, hoping she wasn't so deeply asleep that she wouldn't wake up to listen.

She had sighed, and in her sleep had turned away from him, her hands pillowing her face, her blond hair spread around her. She had looked so lovely, he had just sat and watched her for at least half an hour, mesmerized.

They had had an early breakfast the next morning before she flew back to Washington. Henry reflected on how he had teased her about rejecting him. She had laughed and said that she had always been a sound sleeper, and that was because she had such a clear conscience. So what was his problem? she had asked with a sly smile.

And he had replied that it was all her fault, that he was so crazy about her that sleeping when he was with her seemed like a waste of time. And she had smiled and said, "Don't worry, we have all the time in the world."

He shook his head, struck by the irony of her words. *Oh, Sunday, will I ever see you again?* he thought, giving in to a rare moment of emotional weakness.

Stop it! he admonished himself. You won't get her back by wasting your time. He pressed the buzzer on his armrest. In a matter of seconds, Marvin and Jack were seated opposite him.

He had wanted to leave Marvin Klein in New Jersey, just in case there was any direct contact from the kidnappers, but Marvin had begged to come and Henry had relented. "I have to be with you, sir," Marvin had argued. "Sims will monitor the phones here. He'll keep a line open to us."

Sims, the butler at Drumdoe since Henry's tenth birthday, thirty-four years ago, had said, "You know you can rely on me, sir." He had spoken with his usual calm, even though tears had glinted in his eyes. Henry knew the fondness Sims felt for Sunday.

Now he realized he was glad that he had brought Marvin with him. He had just the kind of analytical, clearheaded approach to problems that Henry so needed at the moment. It was the very trait that, when Henry had been elected to the Senate nearly fifteen years ago, had caused him to elevate the young man from the rank of volunteer.

Without waiting to be asked, Klein said, "No more contact, sir. The operator at the Treasury who took the call was smart enough to go straight to the top, so word of the kidnapping has been contained. So far there has been no hint of a leak."

Jack Collins, Henry's senior Secret Service agent, could have passed for a linebacker on a pro football team. He was a disciplined solid wall of a man, but he too had a definite soft spot when it came to Sunday. The underlying anger and indignation was apparent in his voice when he briefed Henry on what they knew of events so far.

"No one saw the actual kidnapping, sir. Apparently Sunday's . . . I mean Mrs. Britland's car and the follow-up car had somehow been rigged with an explosive device attached to a canister of nerve gas of some sort. It may well have been detonated by remote control, given how quickly the kidnappers were on the scene. Despite the hour, there appear to have been no witnesses, but then the snow had caused a lot of offices and businesses to close early, so traffic was light."

"Do they think that Sunday was injured by the explosion?" Henry asked.

"No, they believe that she, like Art and Leo, the agents who were with her today, was knocked unconscious by the gas, but that the actual explosion was not so large. All that happened to the cars was that they slowed to a stop when the device went off, and the gas apparently immobilized everyone immediately. When our guys regained consciousness, they both could remember only feeling dizzy and then blacking out."

"But how did anyone get to the car in the first place, to plant the gas bomb? Isn't it kept in a safe place?" Henry demanded.

"We're not one hundred percent sure yet, sir. It wasn't a very sophisticated device—actually more like the kind of thing anyone could rig up with a few items from Radio Shack. The gas, of course, is another matter. They are still analyzing that, so we don't know yet where that could have come from. The devices were undoubtedly slipped under the cars when they were parked in the secured parking lot at the Capitol; a simple magnet held each one in place."

"And nobody saw it happen?" Henry asked.

"So far we have come up with no witnesses. They've learned that a guard's apartment was burglarized and his uniform stolen. Part of the problem may be that Mrs. Britland's car itself is so nondescript that it attracted no attention, and it did take right off," the agent said. "Anyone who was around was concentrating on the follow-up car with the two unconscious agents in it."

Henry already knew that Sunday's car with the other unconscious agents in it had been found near the Lincoln

Memorial. Of course, he told himself bitterly, no one would pay much attention to a car that looked as though it had been bought at a repo sale of low- to mid-priced vehicles. His little joke. Forget the limos, he had said. They attract too much attention. No, for Sunday he had had them fix up a state-of-the-art vehicle disguised as "the family car."

My little pretensions, he thought. My little games. Clever, right? Wrong. If Sunday had been in a limo, surely it would have attracted some attention, sitting at the side of the road.

Although the truth was, he knew, that Sunday loved having that kind of car. She would have refused to ever show up at her parents' home in a limousine. Henry realized with a start that in his rush he had failed to contact Sunday's mother and father. I have to do that soon, he decided. They have to know, and they should hear it from me. "Get Sunday's parents on the phone," he told Klein.

It was the most difficult call he'd ever made, but when he hung up after speaking to both of them, the thought that filled his mind was that it was obvious where Sunday got her backbone.

The phone rang, its abrupt sound breaking his reverie. Henry waved aside Marvin's outstretched hand and picked up the receiver himself. It was Desmond Ogilvey; he got straight to the point. "Henry, I'm sorry. Whoever kidnapped Sunday has called CBS. Dan Rather just requested confirmation. He has every detail down exactly, so we know this is the real thing. We've asked him to hold the story for the time being, and he has agreed. But he warned that if there is a leak anywhere else, they will run with it."

"If the kidnapper called Dan Rather, he wants publicity," Henry snapped.

"No, not according to what he told Rather. He said that he was 'testing the integrity of the media,' whatever that means."

"How long ago did the call come in?"

"I'd say less than ten minutes ago. I called you immediately after getting off the phone with Rather. Where are you?"

"Just about to descend into National."

"Well, come directly here. We've got a police escort waiting."

Twenty minutes later, still accompanied by Marvin Klein and Jack Collins, Henry was at the door of the Oval Office. Des Ogilvey was seated at his desk, the presidential seal on the wall behind him. The secretary of the treasury, the attorney general, and the heads of the FBI and the CIA sat in a semicircle around the president. They all jumped to their feet when Henry came in.

It was twenty past six. "There's been another communication, Henry," the president said. "Apparently the kidnappers enjoy toying with us. They called Rather back and said they had decided they wanted him to air their demands. They furnished proof of their sincerity."

For an instant he glanced away from Henry. Then looking directly into his eyes, he said, "Sunday's wallet and a lock of her hair in a sealed plastic envelope were left on the Delta ticket counter at National." Desmond Ogilvey's tone lowered. "Henry, the hair in the envelope was soaked in seawater."

* * *

When Sunday felt the hood being lifted off her head, she had first taken a deep breath and then opened her eyes, hoping to get a good look at her captor. The room was dimly lit, however, and she had trouble making out much of anything. He was wearing a monastic type robe with a hood that fell forward, obscuring much of his face.

He removed the ropes that had held her to the chair. Then, leaving her feet still tied loosely together, he pulled her up to a standing position. Her boots were off, and the concrete floor felt cold to her feet. He was three or four inches taller than she, Sunday noticed. That would make him about six feet. His dark gray eyes, narrow and sunken, had a crafty, malevolent expression, the more frightening because they burned with intelligence. She could feel the strength in his hands and arms as he turned her and said, "I assume you would like to use the facilities."

As she stumbled forward, she struggled mentally to assess her situation. Clearly she was in a basement of some kind. It was desperately cold and filled with the kind of dank smell that airless, sunless basements seem to acquire and retain. The floor was cracked, uneven concrete. The only furniture other than the chair was a portable television set, the rabbit-ear antenna angling from the top.

He held her arm firmly as he led her across the dark room. Sunday winced when a particularly sharp edge of broken cement pierced the sole of her foot. He guided her into a narrow vestibule that led to a staircase; they stopped at a cubicle behind it. The door was open, and inside she could see a toilet and sink.

"You can have your privacy, but don't try anything," he said. "I'll be right outside, holding the door. I searched you, of course, when I brought you in here. I know that women sometimes conceal a weapon or even Mace on their person."

"I'm not carrying anything," she told him.

"Oh, I know that," he said, his tone even. "Maybe you haven't noticed yet that I've relieved you of your jewelry. I must tell you I'm rather surprised that except for a solid gold wedding band, your jewelry is remarkably unexceptional. I would have thought our wealthy former president would have been more generous with his lovely young wife."

Sunday thought fleetingly of the generations of Britland family gems that were now hers. "Neither my husband nor I believe in ostentation or in conspicuous consumption," she replied, encouraged to realize that, beyond cramped limbs and the heartsick worry over Henry and what he must be going through, her temper was steadily rising.

Alone in the tiny lavatory, she splashed water on her face. The hot-water spigot yielded only a sputtering spray, but she was grateful to feel it against her skin. A single bulb that dangled from the ceiling—it couldn't be more than twenty-five watts, she thought—gave just enough glow for her to see in the peeling, film-covered mirror over the sink just how pale and disheveled she was. She had started to turn away when she realized that there was something else, something different about her. What was it?

She stared at her reflection for a few seconds before she realized that a clump of hair had been clumsily cut from the left side of her head, leaving a hole in what had been a very neat trim.

Why did he cut my hair? she wondered.

A chill that had nothing to do with the icy temperature in her basement prison hit the pit of Sunday's stomach.

There was something decidedly alien about her captor. He seemed almost like a robot, programmed to carry out precise, inexorable instructions. A robot but *self*-programmed. He doesn't take orders from anyone. Who was he, and what did he hope to gain from doing this?

There was a tap on the door. "I would suggest you hurry, Congresswoman. There's a broadcast coming up in just a minute that I'm sure you will find interesting."

She pushed against the battered door and it opened. Her monklike captor took her arm in an almost courteous gesture of support. "I wouldn't want you to fall," he said.

As she shuffled awkwardly across the basement, Sunday thought she caught a trace of the scent of bacon cooking. Was there someone upstairs? How many people were involved in this operation? When they reached the chair, the pressure of his palm on her shoulder indicated that she was to sit down.

With quick, deft movements, he again bound her against the chair back, only this time leaving her arms free. "It's 6:30," he said. "You must be getting hungry. But first I want you to see Dan Rather's broadcast. I do hope that for your sake he followed instructions."

The *CBS Evening News* began. A grim-faced Rather reported the breaking story: "Congresswoman Sandra O'Brien Britland of New Jersey, better known as 'Sunday,' the wife of former President Henry Parker Britland, has been kidnapped. Her captor, or captors, are demanding that the international terrorist-assassin Claudus Jovunet be put aboard the new American SST to be flown to some as yet undetermined location. Instructions stipulate that the only other persons allowed on the plane are to be two pilots. If these conditions are not met, the captors say that the congresswoman will be thrown into the Atlantic Ocean. I have spoken with former President Henry Britland, who is in the Oval Office with his successor, Desmond Ogilvey. He assured me that the terms will be met and the government is in full cooperation with the need to ensure his wife's safety."

Sunday's captor smiled. "I'm sure there'll be a lot more about you. I'll just leave it on while I get your dinner. Enjoy the program."

Sunday focused on the TV as Rather was saying, "We're switching live to the White House, where the former president will make a personal plea to his wife's abductors."

A few seconds later, Sunday stared helplessly at the fear and grief in her husband's face. The sound seemed to have changed, and she had to try to lean forward to hear what he was saying.

Then Henry's impassioned plea was drowned out by the sound of singing. There seemed to be two voices, a man's and that perhaps of an old woman. Sunday could barely make out the words. ". . . mice . . ." she heard, and then she understood: "Three blind mice . . . see how they run . . ."

"They all ran after the farmer's wife," she continued mentally.

But that was not what she was hearing. The voices were louder now, and closer, approaching from the staircase.

". . . they all ran after the president's wife, but she'd been drowned for the fish to bite . . ."

The song stopped abruptly. She heard her captor's voice say, "That was very nice. Now go upstairs."

A moment later he was standing before her, holding a small tray.

"Hungry?" he asked pleasantly. "Mother's not much of a cook, but she tries."

Blinking back tears, Henry Britland turned away from the camera. The normally boisterous press room was unnaturally quiet. The eyes of the people gathered there reflected their sympathy.

Looking at him compassionately, Jack Collins mused that if there was one single thought that everyone in the room must be sharing, it was that Henry Parker Britland IV might be one of the nicest, smartest, wealthiest, most charismatic men in the universe, but that everything would be meaningless to him if he lost Sunday.

"I never saw a guy as crazy about his wife," Collins overheard a young White House aide whisper to a young woman at his side. You're so right, Jack thought, so very right. God help him get through this.

President Ogilvey had joined Henry. "Let's go into the Cabinet Room," he said, taking the younger man by the arm.

Impatiently, Henry brushed the last trace of moisture from his eyes. I have to get hold of myself, he thought. I need to concentrate, use my head to get Sunday back. If I don't, I'll have the rest of my life to mourn.

In the Cabinet Room, they sat around the long table as he and Des had done on numerous occasions during his eight years in office. The entire cabinet had joined them now, along with the chairman of the Joint Chiefs of Staff and the FBI and CIA directors.

President Ogilvey deferred to Henry: "We all know why we are here, Henry. You take over."

"Thank you all for coming," Henry said briskly. "Please realize that I understand your feelings as I know you understand mine. Now to the plan of action. I want to say how touched I am that the president has agreed to exchange Jovunet for my wife, and I also understand that we have to make sure that immediately after we get her back we recapture Jovunet. This government cannot be put in the position of caving in to terrorists and hostage situations."

An aide tiptoed unobtrusively into the conference room and whispered in the president's ear. Ogilvey raised his eyes. "Henry, the British prime minister is on the phone. He has expressed his deep regrets and offers any kind of assistance that we feel he could render."

Henry nodded. For a moment his mind flashed back to when he and Sunday were in London. They had stayed at Claridge's. The queen had invited them to a dinner at Windsor Castle. He had been so proud of Sunday. She was the most charming, the most beautiful woman there. They had been so happy . . .

Henry realized with a start that Des was still speaking to him. "Henry, Her Majesty wants to speak to you personally. The prime minister tells us she is deeply concerned. She told him that what they need in her family is a girl just like Sunday."

Henry took the phone that was offered to him, and a moment later he heard the familiar voice of the sovereign of Great Britain.

"Your Majesty . . ." he began.

Another aide was whispering to President Ogilvey. "Sir,

73

we've promised that you would return the calls of the presidents of Egypt and Syria. Both insist that they are unaware of any terrorist organizations within their countries that had anything to do with the kidnapping, and both offer the use of their most elite special task forces in assisting with the congresswoman's safe recovery. Even Saddam Hussein has called to express his outrage and assure us that he knows nothing of who might be behind this incident. He has even promised that if Jovunet is landed in Iraq and Sunday is not safely surrendered, then he will personally see the man beheaded on the spot.

"We've had calls from many other heads of state, sir," the aide continued. "President Rafsanjani even called to say that despite what conclusions anyone might jump to because of what Jovunet said about 'leaving off the caviar,' Iran is in no way involved in this disgraceful episode. So far, Jovunet appears to be a man without a country. Whoever is behind this whole affair has yet to come forward and indicate a willingness to play host to him."

Ogilvey glanced at Henry. They had to get on with this; time was running out.

Henry was finishing up his conversation with the queen. "I am most grateful, Your Majesty, for your expression of concern, and, yes, I promise that one day soon Sunday and I will have the honor of dining with you again."

When he handed the phone back to an aide, Henry looked directly at his successor. "Des, I know what I have to do. I'm leaving immediately to talk to Jovunet. Then we'll fly him here from the prison at Marion. He is the key to all this. Maybe I'll even be able to get some hint as to who is behind it all."

"A very wise idea," the director of the FBI said solemnly. "As I well remember, sir, your negotiating skills are unparalleled." Then, realizing that—particularly in this room—comparisons are considered odious, he covered his mouth and coughed.

The bacon was fried to a fare-thee-well, just short of being totally cremated. The toast, cold and brittle, reminded Sunday of her grandmother's less-than-sterling culinary skills. Granny had always insisted on using an old-fashioned toaster, and she always waited until clouds of smoke signaled that it was time to flip the bread over. Then, when that side had been properly burned, she would scrape the blackened surface into the sink and cheerfully serve the remnants.

But Sunday was hungry, and miserable though the food was, it was at least filling. On the plus side, the tea was very strong, just as she liked it. With its help, her head had begun to clear. The sense of unreality was passing, and now it was beginning to sink in just how very precarious her situation was. This was neither a nightmare nor a bad joke. The man in the monk's garb, either alone or with accomplices, had somehow managed to tamper with her car, which spent virtually all of its idle time parked in a secure area, to disable her very experienced Secret Service agents, and to kidnap her. He—or they—were both daring and very smart.

It must have been shortly after three o'clock when it happened, she thought. Dan Rather came on at 6:30, so it's just a little past seven by now, she decided. That means I've been conscious for less than an hour. So how long have I been here? And how far did we have to travel to get here? Fitting it all together, Sunday decided that she must still be relatively close to the Washington area. Given the weather conditions, her captor could have traveled only so far in spiriting her away from the city.

But where am I? And what is this place? Could this be his home? Possible, she decided. And how many are involved in this operation? So far she had seen only the man in the monk's outfit, and she had heard the voice of what sounded to be an older woman. But that didn't mean that there couldn't be others. It was unlikely though possible that he could have carried out the kidnapping without assistance; this guy was clearly very strong and could easily have maneuvered her body out of her car and into his by himself.

And then the most important question of all registered in her still-foggy mind: What are they going to do with me?

She looked down at the tray with its cup and plate; she was still holding it on her lap. She wished she could reach down and place it on the floor. The dull ache in her shoulder was getting worse, aggravated no doubt by being trussed up with clothesline in a cold, damp cellar. Clearly, though, this was more than a bruise she had suffered. She wished she had let Henry take her for an X ray after she fell off Appleby. Maybe she did have a hairline fracture after all . . .

Wait! I'm crazy, she thought. Here I am worrying about a hairline fracture when I may not be alive long enough for it to mend! They won't release me until that terrorist Jovunet has reached wherever it is he is going. And even when he is safe, what's to guarantee they'll turn me loose?

"Congresswoman."

She spun her head sharply to the side. Her captor was

standing in the doorway of the vestibule. I didn't hear him coming down the stairs, she thought. How long has he been watching me?

His voice had an amused tone as he said, "A little food does wonders, doesn't it? Particularly given the drug I had to use on you. I'm afraid you may be experiencing a bit of a headache, but don't worry, it won't be lasting too much longer."

He approached her. Instinctively, Sunday tried to pull away as he placed his hands on her shoulders. She cringed as she felt them linger, again almost caressing. "Your hair is really very pretty," he said. "I just hope I don't have to cut too much more of it before I convince that husband of yours and all his associates just how deadly serious I am. Now let me relieve you of that tray."

He took it from Sunday's lap and placed it on the television set. "Put your hands behind you," he commanded.

There was nothing she could do but obey.

"I'll try not to make these knots too tight," he said. "And do tell me if your legs start feeling numb. When our man is safely at his destination, it would be quite unfortunate if I had to drag you to your drop-off location, wouldn't it?"

"Wait a minute before you tie my arms behind me," Sunday said quickly. "You have my jacket. It's too cold down here. Let me put it on."

It was as though he hadn't heard her. He continued to pull her arms back. Cords dug into her wrists, sealing her palms together. Sunday gritted her teeth at the sharp flash of pain that cascaded from her right shoulder.

It was obvious that, even in the dim and shadowy light, her captor had seen or felt her reaction. "I don't mean to cause you undue pain," he told her. "I'll ease these ropes a little. And you're right, I know it's quite chilly down here. I'm going to put a blanket around you."

Then he leaned over to pick up something off the floor. Sunday turned her head and bit back a protest. It was the grimy hood she'd been wearing when she awakened in this place. He was being oddly solicitous of her, but she didn't trust him. Something was wrong. She had the sinking feeling that he was just toying with her, that something truly horrible was waiting for her. The thought of that suffocating hood over her again almost made her scream, but she resisted the urge to cry out. She wouldn't give this man the satisfaction of begging.

Instead she asked in the most controlled voice she could muster, "Why do I need that? There isn't much of a view to shut out, and I certainly can't be signaling to any passersby."

Her words seemed to delight her captor. He smiled—a grim, depressing effect—revealing strong but uneven teeth. "Maybe I just enjoy having you disoriented," he said teasingly. "Blindfolds do that, you know."

The light from the dim overhead bulb shone on his hands. Just before the hood slipped over her head, blotting out her vision, Sunday saw the ring he was wearing, a wide gold signet-type design. It looked like many others, except there was a small hole in the center of the ring, as though a stone were missing.

She resisted the urge to take huge gulps of air and forced herself to breathe slowly as the hood settled on her shoulders. As a college freshman, she had gone into therapy aimed at helping her overcome the touch of claustrophobia that she had inherited from her father.

She tried to remember those sessions, but unfortunately the lessons weren't doing her any good now. She could not concentrate on them. The only thing she could focus on at the moment was that ring.

She had seen it somewhere before. But *where?*

It was 9:30 that evening when Henry, accompanied by Jack Collins and preceded and flanked by guards, walked down the long, dreary corridor that led to the small visitor's room reserved for personal contact with the most dangerous criminals in the prison at Marion.

Marion had the reputation of being the toughest of the federal prisons, and Henry had the eerie feeling that it was not so much the screams of the prisoners as of their victims that seemed to permeate these thick, unyielding walls.

Sunday is Claudus Jovunet's victim, Henry thought. And I am his victim, too. The guards ahead of him stopped in front of a steel door. One of them punched in a combination that opened it.

Jovunet was seated at a metal table to the side of the room. Henry recognized him from the pictures that had run in the paper at the time of his capture, and from the interview he had given on *60 Minutes,* a fifteen-minute diatribe of self-aggrandizing arrogance, fortunately balanced by the acerbic wit of Lesley Stahl, who punctured Jovunet's ego balloons every time he tried to float one. Dressed today in a drab prison uniform, a far cry from the dandy attire he had affected when he was still free, and manacled at the waist, hands, and feet, Jovunet nevertheless somehow managed to convey the effect of being at ease and totally comfortable. In an odd way, he also seemed to be totally in control.

His cherubic face showed the beginnings of jowls, his light blue eyes were warm to the point of being merry, his thin, choirboy lips were pink and turned up at the corners, as though trained by constant smiles. To Henry, it was an altogether loathsome visage.

In the plane on the way to Ohio, Henry had read a brief on Jovunet's considerable background. Nobody really was sure of his origin. Now fifty-six, he claimed to have been born in Yugoslavia. He spoke five languages fluently, had begun his career as a teenager running guns in Africa, had been a paid assassin for the highest bidder in a dozen countries, was trusted by no one, and had the ability to radically change his appearance. There were pictures of him that showed him to be easily fifty pounds heavier than he appeared in other photos; there were pictures that showed him looking like a soldier, others like a farm worker, while in yet others he appeared to be an aristocrat.

The one thing that he had not been able to disguise in any of his various personas was his love for designer clothing. It was no small irony that his capture had come while he was attending a Calvin Klein fashion show.

Now as Henry faced him, Jovunet's eyes widened. "Mr. President!" he exclaimed, bowing grandly, leaning forward as much as the restraints would allow. "What a delightful surprise. Forgive me for not standing, but present circumstances do not permit that gesture of respect."

"Shut up," Henry said evenly. His hands were knotted into fists. He wanted only to smash the grin off Jovunet's face; he wanted to throttle him; he wanted to wrap his hands around his neck and choke him until he blurted out where Sunday was being kept.

Jovunet sighed. "And here I was all prepared to help

you. Okay, I give up. What is it you want to know? I realize that many of my past activities are still hidden from the eyes of even your obstreperous media. Clearly this is not a social visit, so obviously you are here because you need me. Perhaps I can be of some assistance. But what do I get in exchange if I help you now?"

"You get exactly what you demanded. Safe passage on our new SST to wherever it is you want to go. We are prepared to make whatever arrangements you require. But you must adhere to our terms in effecting the exchange."

A look of confusion crossed Jovunet's face. "Are you joking?" he asked. Then his expression became reflective. "Very well, Mr. President. Exactly what are your terms?"

Henry felt the solid hand of Jack Collins touch his arm with deliberate force. It was the first time Collins had ever done that. He's telling me to cool it, Henry thought. He's right.

"I am a master pilot and checked out on the SST. I and I alone will pilot you to your destination. You will not disembark until my wife has been released and is safely in the hands of our people. If she is not released both safe and well, the plane will be blown up with both of us on it. Is that clear?"

Jovunet sat in silence for a moment, seemingly absorbing all that he had just heard. "Ah, the power of love!" he said finally, slowly shaking his head.

Henry stared at the man in front of him and realized that the corners of his lips were twitching. Incredulously, he realized that Jovunet was laughing at him. And all that I can do is stand here like a beggar and hope that he will agree, he thought. He saw with loathing that Jovunet's face was glistening with perspiration, even though the small room was cool.

Where was Sunday being held? he wondered. Was it in a cell-like room such as this? It had been a bitterly cold day. Was she warm enough?

Henry forced himself to concentrate on the man in front of him. At least Jovunet was considering the terms he had just outlined. Henry could tell that by his narrowed eyes.

"There is one other consideration," Jovunet said slowly.

Henry waited.

"Like you, I would not want to see anything happen to your wife. I've not had the pleasure of meeting her, of course, but like everyone else in this fair country, I have followed your storybook courtship and marriage. From everything I have heard of her, I would have to say that she is quite admirable. However, as you are aware, given these circumstances, one in my position has only so much control. May I inquire as to the exact time we will be taking off?"

Henry knew that everything hinged on Jovunet believing his answer. "Before my wife was abducted this afternoon, the *Washington Post* reported that a number of mechanical adjustments must be made before the SST's scheduled inaugural flight, set for Friday morning. It will take all day tomorrow to finish them. In place of that intended inaugural flight, you and I will depart on the SST on Friday morning at 10 A.M."

Jovunet looked at him indulgently. "Just think how many cameras and listening devices and satellite chips you'll be installing while you make those mechanical adjustments," he said, sighing. "Ah, well, it won't matter, will it?" His smile relaxed, then disappeared. "I insist on being transferred to the Washington area immediately. And I know you have a number of safe houses around there, so I want to be taken to one of those and not to some correctional facility. I've had enough of this kind of place, thank you."

"That is precisely the plan," Henry said coldly. "You are going to be videotaped while at the safe house, your message to be a warning to your cohorts that my wife must not be harmed. And they must provide us with a videotape of her, showing that she is well; the deadline for that will be 3 P.M. tomorrow."

Jovunet nodded distractedly, then looked down with disdain at his prison uniform. "There is one other small thing. As you undoubtedly know, I rather cherish fine clothing. Since all of my carefully chosen apparel has long since disappeared, and since where I am going is, shall we say, not exactly known for its attention to designer salons, I shall require a complete new wardrobe. I'm particularly partial to Calvin Klein and Giorgio Armani. I want a full and complete wardrobe of their latest fashions, and I will need the presence of several master tailors who will be able to alter them to my specifications by mid-morning Friday. Before we leave, I will have the warden's office supply you with my complete physical dimensions. My new wardrobe is to be transported to the plane in a Vuitton trunk and matching luggage." He paused, then looked steadily at Henry, a slight smile curling his lips. "Do I make myself clear?"

Before Henry could bring himself to respond, Jovunet smiled again, more broadly this time. "Surely none of this should surprise you. Have you forgotten the circumstances of my final arrest? The Calvin Klein fashion show?" He laughed in amusement. "So embarrassing, and it wasn't even a good show. All that underwear! Sometimes I think that dear Calvin is losing it."

Henry knew that he had to get out of there. He could not be in the same room with this man for even ten seconds longer. "I'll see you in Washington tomorrow," he said. He could feel Collins's breath on his neck as they exited. He's afraid I'll kill him, Henry thought. And he's right. As the steel door was closing behind them, Henry heard Jovunet call out one last demand: "Oh, and don't forget the Dom Pérignon and the caviar, Mr. President. Lots of caviar. Even on a supersonic transport, it will be a long flight."

This time Jack Collins had to physically restrain Henry to keep him from rushing back into the visitor's room. Fortunately the door clicked shut, closing off the sight and sound of Claudus Jovunet. "Mr. President," Collins said urgently. "If anything were to go wrong, I swear to you that I'll get him before he has a chance to crawl back here."

Henry wasn't listening, however. "Caviar?" he said aloud. "Something is going on here that has to do with caviar. Any word yet on what country we think is going to be his refuge?"

During the night, Sunday was awakened from an uneasy sleep by a sudden flash of light so bright that it managed to penetrate the thick cloth that still covered her head.

"Just taking your picture," her captor said softly. "You look terribly uncomfortable and forlorn. Perfect. I'm sure your husband's heart will be broken when he has a visual understanding of your predicament."

He lifted the hood from her head. "Now for one more, and then you can go back to sleep."

Sunday blinked in an effort to erase the white spots that blinded her after the second flash. She realized that sometime in the past hours the dim overhead bulb had been turned off; now, as he turned it back on, even that soft glow was painful to her eyes. Her resolve to appear stoically calm shattered. She glared at her captor. "Let me tell you that when I get out of here, *if* I get out of here, you'd better make sure you're on the plane with your assassin friend. And if you are caught, I will go to any lengths to make sure that you are locked away in the most horrible, uncomfortable prison we can find."

Another blinding flash made Sunday blink again.

"Sorry. I hadn't planned that one, but it won't hurt to have your husband see just how upset you are," he said.

No, you are wrong, Sunday thought. I'm not upset, just plain mad. Henry had recently seen her fury at full force when she lectured him on the inhumanity of fox hunting. When she got her Irish up, as he had referred to it, she could be a dynamo.

If that last picture gets to Henry, he will know that I'm not falling apart, Sunday reassured herself.

"It would seem that your husband is moving heaven and earth to secure your safety," her abductor told her. "All the radio and television stations are constantly broadcasting assurances that Claudus Jovunet is being moved to the Washington area, and that a videotape showing him there will be broadcast at 11 A.M. this morning. They have also announced that a videotaped message from you is being demanded. They want to be sure that you are all right."

85

He studied the Polaroid pictures. "Very good. These plus an audiotape should convince your husband and indeed the entire government of the fact that you are both alive and well, although in less than comfortable circumstances."

He dropped the hood over her head again. This time, even though she shut her eyes against the scratchy surface of the cloth, Sunday was keenly alert. She was sure that if she ever hoped to see Henry again she would have to find a way to help herself. She had the strange sense that this guy was playing a deadly cat-and-mouse game with her, and with Henry too. He seemed totally nonpolitical. There had been none of the usual declarations of hatred against the government for imagined crimes, no attempts to justify the actions that had been taken against her in his effort to free Jovunet. Yes, this was like cat and mouse, and Sunday did not like playing the mouse.

But what could she do? Being tied down and kept literally in the dark left her few options. Perhaps physically there was nothing she could do, but her mind could still roam freely. She thought back to the ring she had noticed on her captor's finger. She was positive she had seen it before. But where? And when? Was it on this man's finger, or had it belonged to someone else?

Inch by mental inch she began to consider everyone who might have been that man with the ring. Congressional staff? Ridiculous. Besides the memory seemed to go back further in time. Delivery people? Any of the help at the New Jersey house? No. I've only known Henry less than a year, Sunday thought. And everyone who works for him has been with him forever.

Then who was it?

I'll figure it out eventually, she vowed.

You'd better hurry up, an interior voice cautioned. *You're running out of time.*

Will I ever get out of here alive? she asked herself. Will I ever see Henry again? For a long minute Sunday was shaken to the core of her being. She yearned to be home at Drumdoe with Henry. She had found a wonderful new recipe for garlic chicken in a Provençal cookbook and had intended to try it over the weekend. Working her way through Fordham as a short-order cook had taught her to really love preparing food. She had studied gourmet cooking at the Culinary Institute. Now at least one night of the weekend Henry's longtime *cordon bleu* chef took off and she took over.

She was supposed to be in the House committee meeting this morning. The bill on health benefits for illegal immigrant kids was being discussed again. It drove her crazy that the guy who was leading the fight to deny them benefits was always showing off pictures of his own grandchildren. She had planned to sail into him about that.

But first she had to get out of here, or at least help to get herself out! The Lord helps those who help themselves, she told herself. That had been her father's favorite adage.

And God help those who are caught doing it! That was what I used to think when I was trying to get my defendants off, Sunday thought. Then she inhaled sharply.

That's it, she thought excitedly. I didn't see that ring around Drumdoe or Washington. It does go back further than that. It was when I was a public defender. One of the guys I defended was wearing it.

But which one? Which of the hundreds and hundreds of cases she had tried in those seven years had been the one in which the accused was wearing a thick signet-type ring with a hole in the center?

She was wide awake now, as she thought back over all the cases she had handled. As the last of her mental Rolodex cards flipped over, she shook her head. She was absolutely positive that she had never defended her captor. But she was certain about the ring. Although maybe it wasn't the *exact* ring. Could it be a symbol of a terrorist group? I know I never had a case that involved a terrorist, Sunday thought, and again she reflected on just how nonpolitical this guy seemed. Okay, so he is not a terrorist, and he was never one of my "clients." So who *is* this guy?

Where was Sunday last night? Henry asked himself as he entered the Cabinet Room of the White House at eleven o'clock the following morning. He realized immediately that if anything the mood was even grimmer than it had been at the meeting the previous day. He saw that in addition to Des Ogilvey, the full cabinet, and the heads of the CIA and FBI, two newcomers were present: the Senate Majority Leader and the Speaker of the House. Always looking for a photo opportunity, he thought. Neither man was particularly high on his list.

It had snowed lightly during the night, and the weather forecast was for a major storm to hit sometime before the weekend, probably on Friday. Please God, don't let us be grounded, Henry prayed. The longer Sunday is left in their hands, the more likely the chances of something going wrong.

He thought back to the meeting the night before, with the odious Jovunet. Why the contradiction about the caviar? he wondered once more. It was a small thing, but it had the ring of something significant. Henry had come to the Cabinet Room directly from the safe house where Jovunet, surrounded by tailors, was cheerfully guzzling champagne and beluga caviar. It just didn't make sense that Sunday's kidnappers had made a point of instructing them to eliminate the caviar. Unless, of course, there was some hidden meaning in their message. He shook his head. Despite his years of experience, these games were new to him. Clearly there were no real rules, and anything was possible.

Henry realized that he was standing in front of his designated chair and that everyone was looking at him expectantly. "Mr. President," he said, "I apologize for keeping you waiting."

Desmond Ogilvey, that monument of patience, the president most often compared to "Cool" Calvin Coolidge, said crisply, "Henry, I say this in the hearing of those who will swiftly leak it to the press . . ." He paused to glare at the Speaker of the House. ". . . Don't pull that formal stuff on me unless you're joking. I was born with the highest respect for the government and for statesmanship. But you taught me what the presidency is all about."

And Sunday taught me what happiness is all about, Henry thought.

Desmond Ogilvey folded his hands on the conference table in the exact position the nation's political cartoonists loved to caricature. "I think we are all up to date on the situation," he began. "The SST is being fitted with the most sophisticated equipment in our arsenal. The goal, obviously, is to allow us to monitor Jovunet, so that his future movements will be precisely available to us. If all goes according to plan, as of Friday, if Jovunet is in the jungle, we'll know what tree he's in and even on which branch. Location should not be a problem."

Ogilvey thumped his clenched hands on the conference table. "Here, however, *is* the problem. Despite some significant 'boo-boos'—as my mother used to call them — our two supersleuth agencies are thankfully once again on the ball and in step. All our intelligence agents report unequivocally that no nation, including both our closest allies and our outright enemies, has come forward to offer Jovunet a haven. In fact, virtually everyone has indicated that they would rather see the plane blown up than to see him set foot on their soil. Unfortunately one conclusion we can draw from this situation is that right now, in some country where we don't expect it, a revolution is brewing that will overthrow the existing government and may well present a very real threat to international peace."

Henry listened with a sinking heart. It was as though he were watching Sunday trying to swim in a raging current, and that he was helpless to save her.

"Therefore," Desmond Ogilvey continued, "we must conclude that there is a national emergency pending, that *a nation whose warning signals have been ignored is about to erupt.*" His glance at the director of the CIA caused that unfortunate dignitary to pale. Then the president looked across the table at his predecessor and announced, "I don't know how to say this, but it would seem that your wife, the esteemed congresswoman from New Jersey, is in the hands of an unrecognized foe. I am afraid until they reveal themselves, there is little we can do but wait."

Abruptly Henry stood up. "Des, I've got to revise the statement Jovunet is about to videotape."

He turned to leave the room but was stopped momentarily by the embrace of reassuring arms. "Henry," Desmond Ogilvey vowed, "we're going to get her back. Every facility we can employ is committed to making that happen."

No, Des, Henry thought. We've got to play the game this way, but my gut is telling me that what we're doing is somehow all wrong.

He was becoming unhinged. Sunday could sense the subtle change in her captor's manner. From above the stairwell she had heard him yelling at the woman he referred to as "Mother." Was that woman really his mother, or was that just another part of their ruse? Like the monk's robe, she thought. That disguise looks as though he rented it for a costume party.

The noise from upstairs had awakened her; now she wondered what time it was. It must be hours since he took those pictures, she thought. Would Henry have seen them yet? Would he see the anger in her face and know that she was still fighting to get free? That she was nowhere close to giving up?

She willed herself to ignore the now dreadful pain in her upper arm and shoulder. Why couldn't they be numb like her legs, which she could no longer feel at all. Circulation zero, she thought. If Henry were here, he would . . .

She shook her head. She couldn't think of that. The image of Henry cutting these ropes, lifting her up, gently kneading the circulation back into her tortured limbs—it was too wonderful to consider, and to allow herself the luxury might undo her. She had to be strong. This was a fight, and she wasn't going down without somehow drawing blood.

In her mental review of all the cases she had handled in her seven years as a public defender, she was up to the fourth year. All the *significant* cases, she corrected herself. Dumb kids who punched a bouncer in a penny-ante bar fight were not included in her review.

I'm blessed with a terrific memory, Sunday reassured herself as she shook her head and tried to disengage the rough hood that kept sticking to her forehead. Mom always said I was like her Aunt Kate. "Very observant, never missed anything," Mom explained to Henry when she was filling him in about the relatives. "And nosy. I'll never forget when Kate asked me if I had 'news' for her, clearly asking if I were in a delicate condition. Dear God, I don't think I was expecting Sunday a week, and I had no intention of telling anyone about it yet. I happen to think—"

Sunday had finished the sentence for her. "You happen to think that it's more genteel for a woman to be in her fourth month before she announces it to the world. Maybe your Aunt Kate had a dirty mind. I hear it runs in the family."

But I am like old Kate, Sunday promised herself. I'm an observant, detail-oriented person, and that ring is definitely a detail I noticed in court.

Her reverie was interrupted by the sound of footsteps on the stairs. Sunday felt a nervous quiver go through her body. She wasn't sure what was worse: when her captor crept silently down or when he announced his approach with heavy, deliberate steps.

It had to be morning. She realized she was hungry. Was

he going to feed her? He'd said something about making an audiotape. When was that going to happen?

The footsteps shuffled against the cement floor. Sunday felt the hood being lifted from her head. The robed figure was standing over her. He reached up and turned on the dangling lightbulb, and for several seconds Sunday was once again blinded by the light. When her vision readjusted she stared again at her captor, straining to get any hint of his features. His face was still in shadow, but she continued staring at it, demanding of her subconscious that she recall if she'd seen it before. Sunken eyes, bony facial structure. Probably in his fifties. "Mother should have done a better job," he said angrily. "She left the milk out on the counter overnight and now it's sour. I'm afraid you'll have to settle for dry cereal and black coffee. But first, I'll assist you to the lavatory." He walked around the chair and began to untie the knots.

Mother should have done a better job. . . .

That voice. That tone. I've heard it before. He talked like that to me once, Sunday thought. He said *I* should have done a better job.

Like a developing picture, the memory of it came into focus. It had happened in court, while she was defending Wallace "Sneakers" Klint, just one in the parade of losers she had represented in those early years. Sunday had chosen to be a public defender because she was a staunch supporter of the concept that everyone deserved his day in court. That meant, of course, that everyone deserved full legal representation. The Klint case had been one of her least favorites. Although he was charged with murder, she had succeeded in convincing the jury to find him guilty of the lesser charge of manslaughter, which meant that in twenty years, when he was sixty years old, he would get out of prison.

The trial had not been a particularly long one, in part, she suspected, because the prosecution knew it did not have a very strong case. She remembered that Klint's older brother showed up for a few days of the trial. She looked up again at her captor. No wonder I didn't recognize him, she thought, trying not to let any emotion register on her face. Back then Klint's brother had had long, stringy hair and a beard, and had looked very much like an aging hippie. That's right, he had been very much a part of the "counterculture," something she remembered because there had been some discussion of calling him as a witness, but she had felt that he would probably do more to hurt Sneaker's case than to help it.

Sunday forced herself to think back to the day that he had spoken to her. She had left the courtroom, and he had come up behind her as she was walking down the hall toward the elevators. He had put his hand on her shoulder. She remembered how the ring he was wearing had rubbed against her neck, and that she had yanked his hand away. That was when she noticed the ring's distinctive design.

He had said that the verdict meant a death sentence for their mother, that she'd never live long enough to see Sneakers in her home again. *And that was when he told me I should have done a better job,* she thought.

At the time it hadn't sounded like a threat. In fact, Sunday thought the guy was a jerk; he should have been kissing her feet for keeping his punk brother out of the death chamber. Thanks to her, Sneakers was now making license plates for the state of New Jersey.

So this man was the older brother. And the woman

upstairs had to be the elderly mother. Don't let him know you suspect, Sunday cautioned herself.

But as she tried to fit together the pieces of what she had learned she couldn't make sense of it. What has Sneakers Klint's brother got to do with international terrorism? she kept asking herself. Her kidnapping had seemed so professional, but this guy in front of her seemed more like a lone wacko.

Her arms were finally free. Eagerly she hugged them against her body and tried to massage them.

Her captor was untying the ropes around her legs. When she stood up, she stumbled. Again she searched her memory. His name. What was it? It had been in the court papers. An unusual first name. It began with *W*.

Warfield . . . Woolsey . . . Wexler? That's it! she realized suddenly.

Wexler Klint. She stifled a small smile of victory.

"Here, I'll help you," Wexler Klint said as he put his arm around her waist. She tried not to react when it settled on her hip. Once again he led her to and from the lavatory, then repeated the ritual of tying her to the chair, leaving her hands free until she'd finished what he called breakfast —dry cereal and black coffee.

He stood impassively, watching her as she ate. When she was done, he took the tray with the dishes and spoon, then methodically retied her hands behind her. As he turned to leave he turned on the TV. "Television will make the time pass faster," he said quietly. "Jovunet does his act at eleven." He smiled slightly. "You're still the breaking story, you know. And I suspect you'll continue to be the center of attention for some time to come. Just think,

95

you've now been assured a place in history, and you have me to thank for it."

Sunday did not respond. She was too busy watching Henry being rushed to a waiting helicopter on the White House lawn.

An announcer was saying, "The distraught former president is rumored to be going to the Secret Service facility where Claudus Jovunet is being held. We are told that there has been a change in plans. Instead of a taped message, Jovunet will be seen making his statement on live television. This is to assure Congresswoman Britland's captors that full cooperation with their demands is being given."

Sunday watched as Henry reached the helicopter. He ascended the steps, but before he entered the cabin, he turned to face the cameras. He was handed a microphone. "Pray for her," he said.

Sunday's captor sighed. "Such a nice thought. But it won't do any good, you know."

"Mr. Jovunet, we simply must mike you," Sydney Green, executive media producer for the White House, said impatiently.

They were in Arlington, Virginia, just outside Washington. The charming Federal-style house nestled on acres of gated property was ostensibly the home of a reclusive Mideastern potentate. In actuality it was a safe house for political defectors of significant rank.

The elegantly furnished room was filled with stern-faced CIA agents and government media technicians. Cameras were trained on an as yet unoccupied chair.

Claudus Jovunet stood in an alcove off the main room.

With an air of disdain, he dismissed the beckoning producer. "In a moment. As you can see, I am otherwise engaged." He turned his attention to the tailor who was adjusting the sleeve of a dinner jacket. "I deplore the fact that even fine craftsmen such as yourself have not recognized that my left arm is one half of one inch longer than its counterpart."

"I noticed it. My father and grandfather were master tailors, sir, as am I." Despite the pins in the mouth of the hunched, kneeling clothier, he managed a frosty tone.

Jovunet nodded approvingly. "A man must be convinced of his expertise. I am confident being in your good hands." He nodded to the waiter. Freshly chilled Dom Pérignon bubbled into his glass.

"Put that down and sit down, or I'll personally strangle you," Henry Britland said, his voice deadly quiet.

Jovunet shrugged. "As you wish." He placed the glass on a table and spoke to the tailor. "I think in the interest of time, I must allow you to consider this the final fitting for the evening attire. The rest of the business and sports garments shouldn't take more than a few hours to complete. Following that, we must carefully examine the appropriate haberdashery. I'm pleased to see that you have obtained a number of those marvelously amusing Belois neckties."

Lovingly he picked one of them from the display on a long table and held it out to Henry. "Virtual finger painting, but so sophisticated."

Noting the expression on Henry's face, he returned the necktie to the table. "Yes, the interview!"

* * *

"We have to make our audiotape now. I would say that your husband seems to be getting quite concerned, wouldn't you?" Wexler Klint asked.

Sunday refused to allow herself to dwell on the pained expression in Henry's eyes when with quiet force he had made a statement after Claudus Jovunet smilingly confirmed that he had the promise of the United States government that he would be transported to the destination of his choice, and that he would be flown there on the new SST, piloted by the former president. He would then be allowed to deplane as soon as the safety of Sandra O'Brien Britland had been established. Any misstep on the part of the kidnappers would be fatal for him.

Henry then made his statement saying, "I must emphasize that this trip to freedom for Claudus Jovunet will not begin unless I receive a videotape confirming that my wife is still alive and unharmed. If the trip is to proceed, we must have that tape by 3 P.M. today."

Klint switched off the television and turned to Sunday. He was holding a microphone which was attached to an old tape recorder. He put the microphone almost against her lips and then smiled. "Say something personal that will convince your husband that you were able to watch him and Jovunet just now. Then urge him to cooperate; tell him that any attempt at a double cross will cost you your life. Think about what you want to say. I don't want to have to do this over."

Sunday had already given a lot of thought to what she would say, but that was before she had figured out who her captor was. While she still hadn't been able to piece together just what kind of game Klint was playing, she was confident that he had no intention of keeping any promises to release her. Her mind moved with lightning speed. She took a deep breath. If you ever hope to see Henry again, you'd better make this good, she told herself.

She began to sob. "I don't think I can do this," she told Klint in a little-girl voice. "When I see my husband, I miss him so much. I don't want to be here. I want to be with him."

The dangling lightbulb was casting dark shadows around the gloomy basement, but she could see that the recorder was already turned on. She sighed with resignation. "Okay, you say that I should be sure to mention that I saw him on TV just now." She stopped and sobbed again. She had just hit on the voice she would use, that of the crybaby in her class at St. Al's, the one who had dissolved into tears about three times a day.

"Of course I saw him!" she wailed. "And, Henry, all I could think of was that you'd always promised to defend me. That's why I know you won't let anything happen to me now. You're going to defend me, aren't you, so that I can come home? And, Henry, when I saw you, I noticed that you were wearing the same black English loafers you had on the first time you showed me around Drumdoe. Remember, darling? Oh, there are so many memories. And I still feel so close to you. And I need you so much, I . . ." Her voice broke off in a string of sobs.

Shaking her head, she looked up at Klint. She had managed to squeeze a few tears from her eyes. "Okay, I'm better. Are you ready to start?"

He smiled at her. "No, actually we're finished. You can rest now. I may be a while. Don't go anywhere, now," he said, chuckling as he dropped the hood back over her head.

"You *are* going to let me go once Jovunet has landed

safely, aren't you? I know Henry and the government will keep their promises to you." Then she bit her tongue. She had stupidly used her normal voice.

Klint seemed not to have noticed the sudden shift, however. Instead of a direct answer, he sang, "Three blind mice; see how they run." He adjusted the hood on her head, letting his fingers linger on her neck. Then he put his mouth close to her ear and whispered, "You know who the three blind mice are, don't you? No? Then let me tell you. The first is your husband; the second is the entire U.S. government; the third is . . ." He paused. "The third is Claudus Jovunet."

From the safe house in Arlington, Henry went directly to the newly established command center in the theater of the White House. The slight negative twist of the CIA director's head told him that nothing new had developed. So far all efforts to trace the device used to disable the cars and the Secret Service agents had proved fruitless. And while they seemed convinced that Sunday was still in the general area, no one had come forward with any leads. The bad weather had limited the number of people out on the streets, and apparently no one had seen anything suspicious. The only thing they had to go on so far were a few footprints in the snow, near where Sunday's car had come to a stop. There was no certainty to it, but indications were that they had been left by the kidnapper. Casts of the prints had been made and were currently being checked out.

At the White House, with Jack Collins and Marvin Klein in tow, Henry went to the Cabinet Room where for the fourth time he called Sunday's father at the O'Briens' two-family home in New Jersey.

When he hung up, he said tonelessly, "Sunday's mother and all the aunts and uncles and cousins are in church. Her dad said that his little girl was too smart for even a horde of terrorists. And then he began to cry."

"You've got to eat something, sir," Klein said quietly as he pressed a bell under the table.

"Jovunet certainly hasn't lost his appetite," Collins said bitterly. "Guys tell me he's gone through more champagne and caviar than any of the Russian defectors we've had the pleasure to entertain. They've even had to order more. And now they tell me he wants the chef from Le Lion d'Or to personally prepare his dinner."

"I wonder why he needs to stuff himself now," Henry said, the irritation clear in his voice. "I'm sure they'll have a hero's welcome ready for him, wherever it is he's going." He paused. "Any word yet on where that might be?"

"No, not yet," Klein replied. "The Oval Office might be right—that there is a coup about to take place somewhere and some newly formed government will welcome him—but so far no one has come forward to offer him a new home. Whatever happens had better happen soon; we're running out of time."

Just before three o'clock the cabinet members and others began returning to the Cabinet Room. President Ogilvey and the secretary of state were the last to arrive. "No one, but no one, will admit to having engineered this escape for Jovunet," the secretary said bitterly.

The three o'clock deadline that Henry had imposed came and went as the men sat in silence. At ten minutes past the hour, NBC News anchorman Tom Brokaw phoned the White House with an urgent request to speak to former President Britland. "Put him through," Henry snapped. The Brokaws were frequent dinner guests at Drumdoe.

Brokaw did not waste time on amenities. "Sir, a few minutes ago I received a call purporting to be from a member of what he called the Jovunet Defense and Rescue Squad. At first I thought it was a prank, but the information I was given by our bureau in Washington seems to verify the call. A small package, wrapped in brown paper and addressed to you, was, as promised, found on the floor of the first pew at St. Matthew's Cathedral. We all know how many try to get involved in this type of tragic situation, but this seems to be the real thing. They tell me that under your name on the package, a phone number is printed. Let me give it to you."

"That's the phone number of our villa in Provence," Henry said. "Only a handful of people have it, but, of course, it would be in the book Sunday carries in her purse. Where is the package now?"

"I already instructed our security people to deliver it to you, just in case it might be legitimate," Brokaw said. "It should be arriving at the White House any minute now."

"Tom, you're a true friend. Thank you for not opening it," Henry said earnestly. He stood and handed the phone to Marvin Klein, who was standing right behind him.

"Mr. Brokaw," Klein said, "you know that President Britland is deeply indebted to you. We will, of course, make sure that you are informed immediately of any developments in this terrible situation."

Henry had moved to the door, where he waited impatiently for the package to arrive. At least they seem anxious to let us know that they are cooperating, he told himself hopefully.

"It's an audiotape, sir," Collins said as he entered the room. "But there is a picture with it as well."

His impassive expression had served Henry well during summit meetings, but it failed him now as he looked at the picture. To see Sunday so cruelly bound to a chair in that miserable, shadowy hole was intolerable. Agonized, he noted how tightly her arms were yanked back behind her. Her shoulder had to be killing her, he thought.

But when he looked at her face, he felt almost cheered. He drew some comfort, of course, just from seeing her, just from knowing that she was still alive. There was something else, though, something in her expression that gave him hope. Sunday had to be miserably uncomfortable, but she still had some fight in her. Clearly she hadn't given up. In this picture, she was as mad as Henry had ever seen her.

He looked up. "I want to hear the tape."

Leaning forward on the table, his eyes closed, he listened to his wife's sobbing voice as she pleaded with him to defend her.

When it was over, he said, "I want to hear it again."

He listened through two more times, then glanced up at the moist-eyed men around him. "Don't you see?" he said impatiently. "Sunday's trying to tell us something. The things she's talking about are meant to point us somewhere. I remember clearly the first time I took her to Drumdoe. We were both dressed casually. I wasn't wearing English loafers; I was in sneakers. She's trying to give us a message."

"But Henry," the president said, "she's obviously distraught."

"That's an act, Des," Henry said decisively. "I know my gal. You could put thumbscrews on Sunday and she wouldn't whine like that." He gestured in frustration. "But what I don't know is *what* she's trying to tell us. It must be some kind of clue or a code or something. But what? What in God's name is she trying to tell me?"

Was it still Thursday night or was it Friday morning? Sunday couldn't be sure. She was dozing when she felt her hands being untied.

"I was just watching CNN," Wexler Klint whispered. "They did a big story on you. I didn't know you'd been a lifeguard when you were in high school. Who knows? Maybe that will be useful to you soon." He paused, tying her hands again, but this time in front of her. "Or maybe not. Anyway, we're going for a ride now."

As he spoke, he lifted the hood from her head. Sunday felt a cloth being pulled around her mouth. Her angry protest was first muffled, then silenced. The hood dropped back over her face. Next she felt Klint cut through the ropes that bound her to the chair. As he did it, the knife grazed her right leg, and she felt a trickle of warm blood. Deliberately she rubbed her leg against the chair rung. "Kilroy was here," she thought, remembering the story her father used to tell about how GIs, during the Second World War, would write that message in battle areas.

Hysterical laughter gathered in her throat. *You're losing it,* she told herself. *Calm down.*

But what was he going to *do* with her? she wondered.

She was being lifted, then she felt herself being laid flat

on the rough concrete floor. The smell of stale dampness was almost overwhelming, even through the fabric of the heavy hood. Then she was being wrapped in something, probably the blanket Klint had thrown over her earlier. When had that been? she wondered. Hours ago? Days? Perhaps she could piece it together, but she realized with dismay that she felt almost totally disoriented. She had to get control of herself if she had any hope of surviving this ordeal.

Suddenly she felt herself being lifted, then carried. She was right; he was very strong. He held her in his arms as though she weighed nothing. Her feet brushed against the chair, then against what felt to be a wall. Was he taking her upstairs?

But he turned right, not left. She heard him fumbling at a latch. Then an icy blast of air whipped through the thin blanket. They were going outside. She could hear an engine running.

"I'm afraid the trunk isn't very comfortable," Klint told her, "but we'll just have to make do. Of course, prison cells aren't very comfortable either. I'm afraid that with the road conditions as bad as they are, it will take us at least five hours to get where we're going. But don't worry, we'll be there in plenty of time to witness the drama at National Airport."

Sunday braced her body as she felt herself being dumped into the trunk of the car. He maneuvered her body until she was lying curled up. When she tried to straighten her legs, her feet encountered solid resistance. She felt the blanket being pulled from around her and rearranged until it covered her entire body. The cloth hood flattened against her nostrils, and the knot in the back of the tight gag pressed into the base of her skull. Her shoulder radiated frantic waves of pain. If she had ever been more miserably uncomfortable, she couldn't remember it.

Then she felt things being laid over her. From the sound and feel of it, she guessed that Klint was arranging the contents of the trunk so that she was mostly covered. But he was doing it carefully and quietly, as though he was afraid of being overheard. Where were they? Sunday wondered. Maybe a neighborhood where someone might be standing at a window, watching? From somewhere nearby she could hear a dog bark. Please, God, she prayed, let eyes be on this car now.

Almost silently the trunk was closed. A moment later a jarring lurch was agonizing proof to Sunday that the next phase of her kidnapping had begun.

"Sir, as you know, the Milano sneaker which you wear is an exclusive brand of footwear and priced well beyond the means of the average man." At 5 A.M. on Friday morning, Conrad White, the top-priority CIA analyst was giving Henry Britland an update on their efforts to determine the significance of Sunday's distinctly erroneous reference to the shoes Henry had been wearing the first time he brought her to Drumdoe. As Henry listened, his irritation grew. White somehow managed to convey the impression of delivering a step-by-step lecture to a slow student: *Here is the problem; here are the questions; here are the possible solutions.*

Only you are dead wrong, Henry thought as he listened scornfully. He blinked slowly, trying to reduce the annoying burning in his eyes.

Conrad White noticed: "If I may suggest, sir, even a

few hours' sleep would be advantageous before you undertake what will surely be a long journey."

"You may *not* 'suggest,' " Henry snapped, turning to face the man. "Make your point. I believe what you're trying to tell me is that I was not wearing English loafers and that Milano-brand sneakers are, obviously, Italian made. Therefore your feeling is that my wife's reference is that we are to look to Italy for our abductors."

"Or to one of the troubling sects currently plaguing our Italian friends," White corrected. "Possibly the Mafia. Indeed, *probably* the Mafia. They have a long-standing history of kidnapping and murder. Oh, sorry, sir, I didn't mean to imply . . ."

But he had lost his audience. Henry had turned toward Jack Collins and Marvin Klein. "The East Room," he said abruptly.

He led the way up the staircase from the newly created command center to the main floor, then turned left into the magnificent room, where portraits of George and Martha Washington looked benevolently down on him. Why had he chosen this room? he asked himself as he settled in the chair that had been his favorite when he was the principal resident of 1600 Pennsylvania Avenue. Obviously some instinct was propelling him to it.

Was it because of the wonderful party Des and Roberta had thrown for him and Sunday a few weeks after they were married? he wondered. Cocktails in this room, followed by dinner in the State Dining Room, and then back here for a short concert. Henry thought back to that evening. Sunday had worn a long-sleeved ice-blue satin sheath and the diamond necklace his great-grandfather had bought from a maharajah. She had looked especially beautiful that evening.

Henry almost smiled at the memory of how people had repeatedly said what a pity it was that he hadn't met and married Sunday eight years earlier, since she would have made such a marvelous first lady.

The British ambassador said that to both of us, Henry mused. Then he said something else and Sunday answered him and we all laughed.

You've got to remember, a voice in his subconscious whispered.

Henry leaned forward and clasped his hands together. Maybe White was right; maybe he *was* tired. Maybe this was all his imagination. He shook his head. No, I know there's something here, he said to himself. It's vital that I remember that conversation. I just know that it has something to do with the message Sunday was trying to get across on that tape, he thought with a new surge of hope. *That's why all my instincts told me to come in here . . .*

He realized that Collins and Klein were standing at a respectful distance and waved them to chairs opposite him. "Kind of letting my mind wander, free association. Now it's your turn. Stream of consciousness," he demanded. It was a familiar drill, something the three of them had done together regularly when trying to work out a problem.

Collins went first: "Sir, there's something rotten in the state of Denmark."

Henry felt a surge of new energy burst through his veins. Instinctively he knew that this was going to lead somewhere. "Go on."

"The CIA guys are wasting their time; more importantly, they're wasting *our* time. The Mafia is up to its ears in trouble now that the *omerta* code isn't worth diddley-do. They would *never* take on the United States government by abducting the wife of a former president. Also, sir, there are absolutely no terrorist groups, either new or old, that aren't willing to swear in blood that they're not involved. Nobody ever heard of this Jovunet Defense and Rescue Squad. And also, sir, we can find no record of a terrorist group currently using the word *defense* in its name."

Defense . . . defend . . .

Total recall suddenly struck Henry. It was here, right in this room, he thought, near the portraits of the Washingtons. After the British ambassador had told Sunday how unfortunate it was that she and President Britland hadn't met sooner, Sunday had said, "Back then, I don't think Henry would have given me the time of day. When he was elected president for the first term, I was a second-year law student. Four years later, when he was reelected, I was a public defender, doing battle for my unfortunate clients, some of whom were very deserving, and others I'm afraid, who were not such upright citizens. . . ."

Henry thought: *And then I said that after the stories she's told me about some of those cases, I promised to defend her from any disgruntled clients that she couldn't get off.*

He stood up excitedly, his face flushed. "That's what I've been groping for," he said out loud. He turned to his two startled companions. "Sunday's trying to tell me that somebody from one of her public-defender cases is in on this! Let's go! We don't have that much time."

Sunday knew that being able to fall asleep under virtually any circumstances was an enviable gift. She just hoped it wouldn't work against her this time. However, the bumpy ride assaulted her shoulder so severely that after an hour or so she had utilized the yoga lessons she had taken years ago and forced herself to withdraw from awareness of the pain. Remarkably, she had then fallen asleep.

But that meant she had also lost track of time. How long had they been driving? she wondered. And where were they going? Klint had mentioned National Airport, but since her instincts told her that the house she had been kept in was in the D.C. area, she knew that they would have reached there long before now. No, they were going far away from there.

Even though she couldn't see, she was conscious of the welcome sound of other cars. That meant at least that they had to be on a main road. Would it do any good to try to bang her feet against the top of the trunk? she wondered. No, not unless they stopped for gas or something. But if she was going to take advantage of such an opportunity, it meant that she would just have to endure the pain and stay awake and alert.

In a very short time she sensed that the car was slowing down. Sunday twisted her body, trying to position herself to be able to kick the top of the trunk. They had barely come to a stop, however, before she felt the car start to move forward again.

A toll booth, she thought. But on what highway? In what state? Where were they going?

An hour later she had the answer. When Klint opened the trunk and lifted her out, even through the fabric of the hood and the blanket, she could detect the scent of the ocean.

I didn't know you'd been a lifeguard when you were in

high school. Who knows? Maybe that will be useful to you soon. Klint had said that to her earlier. Now she knew: he was going to drown her.

As Sunday was carried from the trunk, she began to pray silently: "Forgive me for ever feeling cheated, Lord. Most people haven't had even an hour of the kind of happiness I've known with Henry. Take care of him, please. And take care of Mom and Dad, too. No one could have been better to me."

She felt Klint shift her weight onto one arm, then she heard the jingle of a key. A door creaked open. Moments later she was being lowered into a chair.

The continual stabs of pain in her shoulder hadn't abated, but they had lost their importance. Nothing mattered right now other than the fact that she had been given a reprieve. Sunday changed her prayer: "Please, Lord," she whispered inside her soul, "let that Renaissance man I married have the focus he needs to get the message I've tried to send him. Tell him, 'defend' means 'public defender.' Tell him to exchange 'loafers' for 'sneakers.' And then give him the strength to make the leap from there to Sneakers Klint and his crazy brother."

It had taken more than an hour—precious time that they could not spare—to piece together the clues that Sunday had given Henry, but by calling on the combined resources of the CIA and the FBI to help in the search, they had been able to determine which of Sunday's many less-than-sterling clients she might have been referring to with her carefully worded yet still frustratingly obtuse clues. Her use of the word "defend" led them to check through all the many clients she had represented while serving as a public defender. It was her reference to Henry's shoes that had taken the longest to figure out. Finally, by using reverse logic, he was able to deduce that when she spoke of his Gucci loafers, which he had *not* been wearing that day, she was in fact referring to the sneakers he *had* been wearing. It was this leap of comprehension that had finally enabled them to figure out which of her many clients she was referring to: *Sneakers* Klint.

Henry was scarcely inside the room in which Claudus Jovunet was loudly snoring before he began yelling, "Wake up, you bloody assassin. We're through playing games. You've got to talk to us and you've got to talk now!"

Jovunet opened one eye and instinctively reached under his pillow.

"There's no gun there," Jack Collins muttered through clenched teeth. "Those days are over, you jerk." He yanked Jovunet out of bed and pushed him up against the wall. "We want answers. Now!"

Jovunet blinked and wearily smoothed down the sides of his striped Calvin Klein pajamas. "So you've guessed," he said, sighing. "Ah well, I'm sure John Gotti would have done anything to have enjoyed this wonderful day."

Marvin Klein turned on the overhead light. "Talk," he ordered. "Where were you supposed to be taken in the SST?"

Jovunet rubbed his chin, then looked at each of the three men and shrugged. "I don't know."

Henry pushed Collins aside. "Who kidnapped my wife?" he demanded.

Jovunet stared at him.

"Who kidnapped my wife?" Henry shouted.

Jovunet sank down and sat on the side of the bed, rubbing his forehead. "The brandy was definitely a mistake," he said, sighing. "But then I never could resist Rémy Martin VSOP. And the waiter was so very generous with it last night." He looked into Henry's eyes and his expression suddenly became alert. "You know as well as I that no one would give a penny to get me out of prison," he said emphatically. "Over the past thirty-five years there hasn't been a nation or a political group too insignificant for me to double-cross. I'm not especially proud of it. It was just what I did for a living." He paused and looked at the other two men, then back to Henry. "I might as well tell you that had we gone through with it, Mr. President, when you and I got on that plane tomorrow, I wouldn't have known what to tell you. There's nobody out there who wants me. I don't know what kind of game someone is playing with you, but I do know that I have nowhere to go from here. Except back to prison, of course. I'm fully aware of the fact that I'm considerably better off as a permanent resident in Marion, Ohio, than I would be anywhere else in the world. This little day of freedom was a great lark—especially the caviar, which was unbelievable! —and I took full advantage of it because I knew it had to end. I knew you would find me out, and now you have."

Henry stared at the man before him. He isn't lying, he thought, his heart sinking. "Okay, Jovunet, what does the name Sneakers Klint mean to you?"

"Sneakers Klint?" Jovunet looked genuinely confused. "Absolutely nothing. Should it?"

"We have reason to believe that he may be involved in the kidnapping of my wife, or more likely that his older brother, Wexler Klint, may be involved. Sneakers Klint is currently serving time in prison. His brother has never been convicted of anything, but we think he may have a grudge against my wife."

Jovunet shook his head. "I'm sorry to disappoint you, gentlemen. I've known many unsavory characters in my time, but unfortunately your Mr. Sneakers Klint and his brother are not among them."

A couple of hours later, as the morning sun struggled to penetrate the somber clouds that seemed determined never to go away, the atmosphere inside the command center at 1600 Pennsylvania Avenue crackled with electricity.

The president, dressed in his favorite casual clothing, jeans and a Fred Imus Auto-Body Express denim work-shirt, had just emerged from his private quarters two floors above and was standing next to Henry, who had taken an alternating sizzling-hot and ice-cold shower in an effort to clear his head. One of the Secret Service entourage had gone to the former president's Watergate apartment and returned with aviation gear as well as a turtleneck sweater and slacks. Henry had also shaved, for the first time in two days. The shave and fresh clothes were concessions he made only because he kept telling himself that today they were going to find Sunday, and he didn't want to be so grungy when he was reunited with her.

Another CIA analyst had joined Agent Conrad White, who had earlier advanced the Mafia theory to explain Sunday's kidnapping. The two men were arguing quietly about the modus operandi to be followed, when they noted the former president approaching.

White, who continued to advance his case for Mafia involvement, turned to Henry as he joined them. "Sir," he said earnestly, "Sneakers Klint was always on the fringe of the mob, a small-time hood who frequently did jobs for them. I strongly feel that his brother may also have been in their employ. The probability is that they found Wexler Klint too much of a loose cannon. Your insistence that we retrieve Wexler's juvenile records has proved very valuable. As a youth he was involved in many scrapes. He seems to have embraced the hippie culture of the late sixties and for a time was suspected of involvement with the more radical underground groups, although our impression is that his lack of association with any college at the time made him anathema to them, so he was never actually granted membership. The last item on his official record, however, is the most telling. It appears that someone claiming to belong to the SDL—one of the most violent of the campus groups—left a letter on the Pan Am ticket counter at Newark Airport, threatening to kidnap the mayor of Hackensack, New Jersey. Wexler Klint was one of the suspects, but the case was never solved.

"After that, except for the occasional traffic violation and a couple of disturbing-the-peace citations, Klint's name disappears from the police records. We do know, however, that he held numerous jobs. His IQ is near genius. That, coupled with the fact that he once worked at a plant where he mixed chemicals in the manufacture of deodorant and later worked as an auto mechanic, we feel—"

"Why are you going on like this?" a clearly frustrated Henry Britland asked, his voice pitched at a dangerous level. "None of this matters. We know who our man is."

"But sir," White interrupted, "we have to—"

"You have to help me find my wife. Once you do that

you can analyze the situation all you want to. Do I make myself clear? I don't want a psychological profile; I want a plan of action." He paused, his face now only inches from the startled CIA man's. "Now, have you two agreed on a common strategy?"

The analyst who had been silent during White's explanation responded. "With all sympathy for the plight of Mrs. Britland and for your frustration, I'm afraid that all we can do is give you our best estimate of what we think Klint might be thinking and what he might respond to." He paused, nodding toward White. "My colleague and I both feel that we should announce to the media that we know that the man we are looking for is Wexler Klint, and make part of that announcement the government's promise that he will be given safe and careful treatment when he surrenders, and, of course, safely returns your wife."

"You both agree on this?" Henry demanded.

White spoke up again. "Except I feel that there is obviously a strong family feeling between the Klint brothers, and that an added inducement to surrender peacefully might lie in our promise that the two brothers be given visitation rights to each other's prisons."

The suggestion hung in midair as Henry continued to stare at the man.

With a look that expressed both disgust and incredulity, he left the two men and crossed the room to where his successor was talking with several others. "Des, we've got to get going. I have a terrible sense that we don't have a lot of time. We haven't heard from this creep in hours. There is no telling where Sunday could be by now." He turned to Marvin Klein. "Marv, isn't there any word yet on where Klint may have been living?"

"Not yet, sir. Our people are grilling Sneakers in the state prison in Trenton, but he keeps insisting that he doesn't know where his brother is. Says that he hasn't seen or heard from him since that last day in court. Unfortunately, the men I spoke to there think that he may be telling the truth."

Jack Collins spoke up. "What we do know is that the family no longer lives in Hoboken, where they were when Sneakers was convicted. We found that place. It would appear that gentrification caught up with them and they were forced out. Sneakers was able to tell us that his mother had an ailing sister in the D.C. area who had her own house, and he suspects his mother may have moved there. As for his brother, he said that he always had grandiose schemes about 'getting even' with the government for all sorts of wrongs he felt he had suffered, and of doing something that would get him into the history books. He said that their mother had always been a little nuts, and he thinks his brother may be that way too." Collins shook his head. "Anyway, we are checking out the D.C. lead, looking for some record of the sister and where she might live."

From across the room there came a shout of exultation. "Sir, we've located the sister's house. She apparently died recently, but we think the Klint brothers' mother is there, and very probably Wexler Klint as well."

"Let's go!" Henry shouted. "I bet that's where we'll find Sunday."

Twenty minutes later, a dejected Henry Britland stood in the basement of a rundown Georgetown house. In his hand he held Sunday's jacket. The chair in which she had been photographed had the ends of ropes still tied to the rungs and back. He watched as the agent who had been photographing the area suddenly stopped and squatted down beside the chair.

"What is it?" Henry demanded.

The agent hesitated. "I'm afraid it's blood, sir."

Heartsick, Henry visualized what had happened. Carelessly cutting the ropes that held Sunday to the chair, her kidnapper had sliced her leg. His body shaking with rage, the former president turned away. I will kill him, Henry silently vowed. I will find him, and I will kill him.

Jack Collins examined the smear of blood. "Sir, I wouldn't worry about this too much; given how little actual blood there is, I would suspect that the cut is superficial. It almost looks as though she may have intentionally smeared the blood here." He straightened up. "Sir, it's nine o'clock. What have you decided to do?"

Henry clenched and unclenched his hands on the tweed jacket that still held the faint hint of one of Sunday's favorite scents. "I want to talk to the mother."

"You won't get much out of her, sir. She's frightened and confused. All she seemed to be able to tell us is that her son brought a lady home, but that he wouldn't let her go down to the basement to meet her."

Henry found the elderly woman sitting on a dilapidated couch in the small living room of the narrow row house. Her face had a faraway, vaguely sad look to it, and she sat rocking as she hummed softly to herself.

He sat beside her and took her hand. Rich or poor, he thought, it's all the same when your mind is going. His own grandmother had suffered from Alzheimer's disease.

Remembering how he had spoken to his grandmother, he took Mrs. Klint's frail hand in his. "That's a nice song you're humming," he said. " 'Three Blind Mice,' isn't it? Why are you singing that?"

She looked at him. "Everybody's angry at me," she said.

"No one's angry at you," Henry said, his voice comforting. He felt the tension in her hand begin to ease.

"I spoiled the milk. My son told me to sing along with him. But then he got angry with me. I spoiled the milk."

"That's not such a bad thing. He shouldn't have gotten mad," Henry told her. "Where is your son now?"

"He said he was taking his lady friend swimming."

Henry felt his throat tighten with sudden fear. The envelope with Sunday's hair soaked in seawater—of course, he should have made the connection. He managed to ask, "When did he take her swimming?"

"They're going swimming when the plane takes off. I wanted to go too, but he said it was too far. Is New Jersey far away? I'm from there, you know."

"New Jersey," Henry said. "Do you know where?"

"I know where. But it's too far." She paused and looked at her hands. "Is Long Branch too far? I liked it there. I liked my house there better than the one we had in Hoboken. It was close to the ocean. After the plane goes away, they're going swimming." She closed her eyes and began to hum again.

Patting the woman's hand, Henry stood up. "Be gentle with her," he directed the agent at the doorway. "And for God's sake, sit next to her, keep talking to her, and *listen* to her."

* * *

At ten minutes before ten o'clock, from a secure distance, television cameras recorded the procession of dozens of Secret Service agents escorting the former president of the United States, Henry Parker Britland, and terrorist Claudus Jovunet across the tarmac to the waiting SST.

When they reached the steps, the agents stood back and watched as Britland and Jovunet ascended the steps alone and then closed the plane's door behind them.

"Jovunet has informed the government that he will not disclose his destination until he has been served brunch," Dan Rather informed television viewers. "The menu he has demanded includes oysters on the half shell, a caviar omelet, chateaubriand with asparagus, and a selection of pastries, accompanied by suitable vintage wines, all to be followed by fine port. The chef from Le Lion d'Or boarded the plane earlier to make preparations and will, of course, deplane when service is complete. The former president will then file his flight plan and they will be off.

"We have been told of no further word from the captors holding Mr. Britland's wife, Congresswoman Sandra O'Brien Britland, but our sources indicate that they expect her to be released only when the plane has landed at its yet-to-be-announced destination.

"And so," Rather went on, "the drama continues to unfold. Through the courtesy of a viewer, we have been fortunate to receive home-movie footage of Congresswoman Britland as she appeared in her fourth-grade dance recital. We are pleased to share that with you now."

Oh my God, Sunday thought as she viewed herself prancing about on a stage, wearing a green tutu and carrying a sparkling wand. They've got to be kidding.

Her head had still been covered when Klint brought her here, but they appeared to be in yet another cellar, although, if possible, this one seemed even more seedy. Klint had brought his television set with him and had plugged it into the same outlet the dim bulb was hanging from.

The metal chair she was tied to had sharp, rusty edges, but she was beyond caring. The only thing that mattered was that Henry had picked up her message. She was positive that had not been Henry in coveralls and flight jacket. It probably was the agent who sometimes used to stand in for him when they wanted people to think they had seen the president board a helicopter headed to Camp David.

She also recognized the talk about brunch as being a stall tactic. But did Wexler Klint suspect anything? Cautiously she glanced to the side of the room where he sat sprawled on a moldy mattress, the monk's robe beside him. He had changed into a wet suit, and kept impatiently plucking at the tight-fitting material.

Sunday fought back the sense of rising panic. If Henry followed my clues and went to my old files, Sneakers's name would have popped up, she thought as she struggled to reassure herself. I'm certain he's looking for me right now. Otherwise he would be on that plane.

Some fifty miles away, Henry's private helicopter was circling over Long Branch, New Jersey. Dozens of agents were swarming over every inch of oceanfront property. Others were ringing doorbells and searching every house that appeared to be empty.

"Sir, if she's here, we'll find her," Marvin Klein said for the fifth time in less than half an hour.

"But if there was any semblance of reality in what that

poor old woman said, then why can't we find any record of them living here? There's no record of a deed registered to Klint in or even near Long Branch," Henry said, the frustration showing in his voice. "The whole thing could have been just a figment of her imagination."

Time is running out. Time is running out, he said over and over in his mind. There isn't a shred of evidence to indicate that this is anything other than a wild-goose chase. Klint could have her on a beach as far away as North Carolina by now. They might not have even owned a house here; they might have just rented. Or they might have used a different name. We just don't have time to follow up on all the possibilities.

"Get me Trenton State Prison on the phone," he said to Klein. "I want to speak to Sneakers again."

As time passed with absolutely nothing happening, newscasters were reduced to repeating the known bits of the crisis over and over again. The camera remained focused on the SST sitting on the distant runway.

"Now that it's almost noon, the brunch must be nearly over," Tom Brokaw informed his viewers. "We should see the chef emerging from the plane any time now." What he didn't say was that he, along with many other experienced newsmen, had begun to suspect that this was merely a delaying action.

"If that plane doesn't take off by 12:30, you won't be around to wave bye-bye to your husband," Wexler Klint said angrily. "I'm tired of this. I'm starting to think that they're playing with me." He stood up and walked to the cellar door and looked outside. "Getting cloudy again.

Real windy, too. That's all to the good. No one'll be out on the beach today."

He left the room and returned with an old-fashioned alarm clock. He wound the noisy mechanism and set the hands to the proper time. Then he set the alarm. Placing the clock on the floor in front of her chair, he looked at Sunday and smiled. "At 12:30 you and I take our swim."

Claudus Jovunet finished the last of the caviar he had brought with him to the plane. There was, of course, no actual chef on board the SST, just the former president's stand-in and a bunch of federal agents, including the one who had impersonated the chef for the benefit of the media. Nonetheless, he had enjoyed the repast he had been able to scrape together from yesterday's leftovers. "My, my, my, how I do miss the good life," he said with a sigh. He looked with longing around the comfortably appointed plane cabin. Then his gaze turned to the Vuitton luggage, which held his beloved new wardrobe. Since it was part of the whole ruse, the agents had acceded to his request that it be allowed to accompany him on board.

"Do you suppose that when they return me to Marion, in gratitude for the cooperation I have given them, they might allow me to keep the Belois ties?" he asked Henry's stand-in.

"Mr. President, if I could help you, I would," Sneakers Klint said plaintively. "I mean, these guards here ain't always the easiest people to get along with, if you get my drift." He paused. "Look, here's all I know. Mama had Wex when she was forty-three, me when she was forty-five. Our dad? Who knows? I never knew him, and Mama never talked about him. Ran out sometime right after I came along, I guess."

"I'm aware of your family history," Henry said, anxious to learn something, anything new.

"But I wanna reiterate again—'cause it wasn't Mama's fault. Wex and I both kinda got in with a bad crowd, but Mama tried. She made us go to school, and for a while Wex even hung around with some college types. We was both smart, and I mean *smart*. But hey, what can you do? Right?"

"Look, did your mother ever own a house in Long Branch, New Jersey?" Henry snapped. "That's all I want to know."

"Listen, Mama's pushing ninety. Give her a break. She didn't know if I was going to prison or off on a Carnival Cruise. She's out of it. So's my brother, of course, only he can't blame it on old age. He's just plain nuts."

"Stop it," Henry said, nearly shouting now. "I don't care! All I want to know is if your brother might have had a place in Long Beach."

"You said Long Branch before. Which did you mean?" Sneakers said. "As a matter of fact, we did used to go to Long Beach Island. Wex and Mama liked it there. I've been thinking. He always was saying that someday people were going to know who he was. Always had harebrained schemes for doing something that he said would make him go down in history. He once got into trouble because he threatened to kidnap the mayor of Hackensack...His name was—get this—Obie Good. Short for Obious Good. What a moniker, right? Wex always used that dopey name as a sue-de-nim. O-period B-period Good."

Henry had stopped listening. *Long Beach Island.* I wonder if Mrs. Klint could have made the same slip? At least she has a good excuse, he thought.

Long Beach Island was only fifty miles or so south of Long Branch, but it might as well have been a thousand given how little time they had left.

He scrawled a note to Marvin Klein. It ready simply, "Long Beach Island. Check listing for O. B. Good."

Ten seconds later the entire fleet of helicopters had turned south, rushing to cover the distance between Long Branch and Long Beach Island, New Jersey. It was 12:28 P.M.

Dan Rather was on camera this time, with the shot of the SST appearing on a screen behind him. Clearly it still sat on the runway, and there seemed to be no activity anywhere around it. He shuffled a few papers he had in front of him, then looked to his right as if to check for instructions. Turning back to the camera, he said, "Well, our latest information is that the flight plan has been filed, but that an unexpected glitch in the engines has delayed the departure of the aircraft. President Desmond Ogilvey is about to make a personal appeal to the abductors of Congresswoman Britland, requesting that they be patient and give the ground crew time to take care of this mechanical problem."

The television was now the only light in the dank basement room at the New Jersey shore. The sound of President Ogilvey's voice made a hollow sound as it bounced off the walls of the room. There was no one there to hear him.

* * *

T. S. Eliot wrote that the world doesn't end with a bang but with a whimper, Sunday thought as she was shoved and prodded across the beach to the ominously gray Atlantic Ocean, but I'm damned if I'm going to whimper now! Her arms were tied in front of her, and while her feet were still tied together, there was enough slack in the rope to allow her to hobble through the sand. Propelling her was Wexler Klint, now fully encased in his wet suit, complete with diving mask and air tank. He had his arm around her and was rushing her toward the water's edge.

It's got to be freezing in there, Sunday thought. Even if I had a chance, I wouldn't have a chance. I'll end up with hypothermia. Or do I mean hydrothermia? Oh, Henry, I thought I'd do something with my life. I thought I'd do good things for deserving people and then come home to you. It would have been so wonderful, and I am so sorry to miss it.

They had reached the water's edge, and she felt the icy surf hitting her feet.

Oh God, it's so cold, she thought, her alarm growing.

A wave splashed around her knees.

From the time I was a little kid, I always loved the ocean, she remembered, thinking for a moment of herself as a little girl at the Jersey shore, always heading toward the water. Mom used to say she needed eyes in the back of her head to keep track of me on the beach, she thought. I could sure use those eyes on me now. Good-bye Mom; bye, Dad.

She was up to her waist in the swirling water; the undertow was starting to drag at her feet. "Henry, I love you," she said to herself.

His eyes distant and mechanically cold, Klint continued

to force Sunday out farther and farther from the shore. The tight seal of the wet suit and the roar of the water kept him from hearing the faint drone that approached from the northern end of the beach, growing louder by the second.

It was Wexler Klint's plan to drag Sunday into deep water, drown her far from shore, then float her body far enough out to be caught in the fast-moving current. It might wash up somewhere in a few days, or a month, but what difference would it make? She would be dead, and that was all that mattered. He didn't even care if he got caught eventually. He would make his mark. He would have his place in the history books.

"Sir, to the left! Look!"

Henry rushed to the other side of the helicopter. Through his binoculars he could see a figure out in the water, at least twenty yards from shore. He adjusted the focus, trying to get a clearer view. The figure appeared to be holding something down. He couldn't make out what was happening, if maybe this might just be a lone fisherman intent on getting his catch at any cost. Time was too precious to waste it on the wrong thing.

They were getting closer. He adjusted the focus once more; then he finally saw it: blond hair, floating on the churning surface of the water! *Sunday,* he thought. *That has to be Sunday!* "Dive!" he shouted.

The helicopter began its rushing descent.

Tightly held by Klint, Sunday was struggling, but she could not keep her head above the water. *Good-bye, Henry,* she thought.

It was then Klint heard the roar of the approaching

helicopters, looked up, and realized what was happening. Frantically he wrapped his arms around Sunday's neck and pulled her under the water. He still had time to finish her. Even though he'd be caught, he'd have his place in the history books. He'd show those jerks. How much he hated them.

Those jerks in Washington.

It was Wexler Klint's last thought before he woke up some minutes later, firmly in custody.

Henry's cannonball plunge into the ocean allowed him to spring immediately back to the surface. He grabbed Sunday in one arm. With the other, he ripped Klint's face mask off and squeezed his neck in a paralyzing pinch. I hope he drowns, Henry thought. Helicopters deposited a fleet of agents into the water around them.

"My love, my love," Henry said over and over to Sunday as he swam through the breakers, towing her beside him.

"Henry, darling," a shivering Sunday whispered back as she wrapped her arms around his neck. "Don't dare kiss me until I have a chance to brush my teeth."

In his entire life, Henry Parker Britland IV had hardly ever told anyone to shut up, but he came perilously close at that moment. He was also perilously close to tears as he reached the beach and rolled onto the sand, holding his beloved Sunday cradled in his arms. Ignoring her request, he kissed her lips and whispered, "Do be quiet, darling."

He was rewarded by a faint giggle, emerging through chattering teeth.

He looked into her eyes. Hysterical, he thought. "Let it

out," he said soothingly. "You've had a terrible time." Then added incredulously, "By God, you're *laughing!*"

"Oh, it's not at you, darling," she said, burrowing her face against his neck as a wave washed over them. "I was just thinking that this is a crazy time of year for us to be playing Burt Lancaster and Deborah Kerr."

"What are you talking about?" Henry asked, bewildered.

"From Here to Eternity."

Hail,
Columbia!

In the Ecuadoran Restaurant Mendalez's Plaza, El Viejo
Cosizo Ronabres, a white-haired man in his ninth
decade, followed others to read the newspaper item
aloud and then toasted again from his own bottle.

They were squint and window side still looked on an
Central Park, and the backyard caniques knew the way
your hearing went cub-tripping up into the quietly
elegant prow. As he waited for his arguments, Regnery bit
on mints, making up to fortified her filth. As a paint artist,
he'd wondered how she put full when turned, how flex
f-dom ...

The *receptionist* stationed was exactly, sharply, but
expected thinground measurement. Jon was slowly returned
to the saloon...

With the large 50' Gallery table-court he couldn't, the
...

THE NEW YORK TIMES. November 8

Former President Henry Parker Britland IV has purchased the yacht *Columbia,* reclaiming ownership for
his family. Built for the Britland family and launched
in 1940, the *Columbia* was sold in 1964 to the late
Hodgins Weatherby. Just prior to that sale, the vessel
had been the scene of the mysterious and still-
unsolved disappearance of Costa Barria's Prime Minister Garcia del Rio.

In the three decades after it passed out of Britland
hands, the yacht acquired the reputation of being
haunted, due in part to the disappearance of Mr. del
Rio and in part to the rather eccentric and at times
controversial behavior of her most recent owner.

Larger and reportedly far more luxurious than the
onetime official presidential yacht *Sequoia,* the *Columbia* has been a favorite retreat for presidents from
FDR to Gerald Ford.

In the Edwardian Room of Manhattan's Plaza Hotel, Congor Reuthers, a thin, muscular man in his fifties, tremblingly followed orders to read the newspaper item aloud and then looked up in fear at his employer.

They were seated at a window table that looked out on Central Park, and the horse-drawn carriages across the way were sending faint clip-clopping sounds into the quietly elegant room. As he waited for a response, Reuthers had an instant flashback to his first fox hunt. As a young lad, he'd wondered how the fox felt when trapped. Now he knew.

The reaction that unfolded was exactly what he had expected: His employer's coffee cup was slowly returned to the saucer.

Even the china-blue contact lenses could not conceal the searing fury in her frosty black eyes. As usual, Angelica was traveling incognito. Presently she was in her Lady Roth-Jones disguise, wearing the blue lenses, a severe dark blond wig, a tweed suit, and oxfords.

When she continued to stare at him, Reuthers dropped his eyes. "I'm sorry," he mumbled, then wished he'd bitten his tongue.

"You're sorry." The tone was level. "I would have hoped for a more appropriate response. Where was Carlos?"

"He was there, as ordered."

"Then why didn't he bid for the yacht? No, not *bid;* why didn't he *buy* the yacht?"

"He was afraid that one of the Secret Service men might recognize him. No one knew that Britland was planning to be there. We had not anticipated the competition. Carlos rushed out to send for Roberto to do the bidding. By the time Roberto could get through security, President Britland had tripled the opening bid. An instant later the yacht was his. The proceeds were going to charity, you see . . ."

His employer stared at him in silence for several moments, then asked, "What are Britland's plans for the yacht?"

This time Reuthers would have preferred to swallow his tongue rather than answer. "He is said to be sailing on it immediately to his private marina in Boca Raton, Florida. He has an architectural degree, as you know, and it is said that he plans to redesign the interior himself, then present the yacht to the government so that once again it will become a retreat for visiting heads of state. With the gift, there apparently will be a sizable endowment for maintenance."

"We know what *that* means."

Reuthers nodded dumbly.

"Neither Carlos nor Roberto is useful to me any longer." Fingers that previously had held the delicate china coffee cup were suddenly convulsive as they gripped the edge of the table.

"Surely . . ." Reuthers closed his lips to stifle the protest.

"Surely?" A venomous whisper mocked him. "Be careful you don't join your friends. What use are you to me? *You* should have known that Britland was planning to bid on the *Columbia.*" The hard eyes glared at Reuthers with heart-stopping coldness. "Get out of my sight!"

"Henry, darling, I still can't believe it," Sunday sighed as she pressed against the railing of the *Columbia,* straining to catch the first glimpse of Belle Maris, the Britlands' oceanfront Florida estate. Craning her neck, she brushed breeze-blown, wheat-colored hair from blocking the view of sparkling blue eyes.

"My fairest, my espoused, my latest found, Heaven's last, best gift, my ever new delight!" Henry Parker Britland IV mused as he looked up from the lounge chair on which he was stretched out, studying the blueprints of the *Columbia*. Since Sunday's recent abduction, these tender words of Milton had come frequently to mind.

"Why don't you believe it?" he asked affectionately.

"Because when I was nine, I read a book about the *Columbia* and tried to imagine what it must have been like when President Roosevelt and Winston Churchill sailed down the Potomac on her. Can you imagine the conversations they had? And President Truman used to play the piano for his guests when he and Bess had a party here. And the Kennedys and the Johnsons loved this boat, and did you know that President Ford used to practice his golf swing on the foredeck?"

"He hit the captain, once," Henry observed dryly. "In fact, the joke was that the staff received combat pay when President Ford got out his golf clubs."

Sunday smiled. "I should have realized you are aware of everything about the *Columbia*. You practically grew up on her." Her expression became serious. "And I *do* know that you've never forgotten the night Prime Minister del Rio vanished. And I can understand that. We're still living with the ramifications of his disappearance."

"I was twelve," Henry said somberly. "And the last person to speak to him before he went out on deck for a smoke. The most charming man I've ever known. He had asked me to walk with him."

Sunday could see that her husband's eyes grew clouded and sad. She walked over to the lounge chair and perched on the side.

Henry moved his legs to give her more room and reached for her hand. "Since I was the sole member of this generation of Britlands, my father included me on every possible occasion. Good heavens, I even flew with him to visit the shah, during the heyday of the monarchy in Iran."

Sunday never tired of hearing Henry's stories about his adventures as a child and young man. It was so totally different from her own experience of growing up in Jersey City as the child of a motorman on the New Jersey Central.

Now, keen as she was to find out what had happened when Henry visited the shah, Sunday was more interested to learn what had happened on the *Columbia* that night. "I didn't know you were the last one to actually speak to Prime Minister del Rio," she said quietly.

"The dinner had been very pleasant," Henry said. "The prime minister had announced Father's plan to send his engineering company to build a series of bridges and tunnels and roads in Costa Barria, half of the cost to be his personal gift to the country. It would have drastically improved the economy. Everyone in that room realized that the economic boom would mean del Rio would be able to hold onto power absolutely and thus keep Costa Barria from sliding back into a dictatorship."

"Del Rio and his associates must have been extremely happy," Sunday said. "Do you believe it's possible that he committed suicide?" Noting the frown that suddenly clouded her husband's forehead, she added, "Henry, darling, I think I know how painful it is for you to talk about this. So feel free to tell me to take a hike."

Henry raised his eyes. "Sweetheart, if you took a hike, you'd have a pretty good swim to shore. And even though you haven't mentioned it—*yet*—I do know that you haven't decided on your vote on the bill before Congress that would resume aid to Costa Barria."

Defensively, Sunday said, "I know you believe it would be better to continue to keep the squeeze on, but it is hard to ignore an island with eight million inhabitants, many of whom live in poverty and who desperately need our help."

"Bobby Kennedy gave a version of that argument concerning the opening of China."

"In 1968, wasn't it?" Sunday asked.

"June of 1968, to be exact," Henry replied. "As to the prime minister, he was a great friend of my father and had visited with us regularly. I'm proud to say that he had taken a liking to me, and since I had made it my business to learn everything I could about his country, including the political situation as well as the economics, he enjoyed quizzing me. On that last day, he and I had been swimming together in the outdoor pool. It was a beautiful afternoon, but he seemed melancholy. And then he said something very odd. Quite somberly, he told me that for some reason Caesar's final words had been haunting him."

" '*Et tu, Brute?*' Why on earth would he say that?"

"I don't know. He lived with the possibility of assassination, of course. It was a constant. But on the *Columbia* he'd always felt secure. However, I *do* know that he was subject to spells of depression, and from what I understand now, that constant apprehension may have gotten to him that evening."

"That's possible," Sunday agreed.

"As I mentioned, the dinner was quite enjoyable and ended at quarter past ten. Madame del Rio retired immediately, but the prime minister stayed behind to exchange pleasantries. Then, as I was leaving the dining room, he appeared at my side and invited me to stroll around the deck. I replied that my mother expected me to phone her at ten-thirty. Mother was entertaining her old friend Queen Juliana of the Netherlands, who was visiting New York that week. Then, looking at his face, I realized that beneath the genial manner, del Rio was deeply troubled. I quickly told him that Mother would be honored for me to accept his invitation and accompany him."

"Then you can't blame yourself," Sunday insisted.

Henry stared past her into the sea. "I remember that he patted my shoulder and said that I must not disappoint my mother, that perhaps I had made the best choice for both of us. He said that he needed to be alone, that there was something quite urgent he had to think through. Then he embraced me and in the same gesture surreptitiously took an envelope from his pocket and slipped it into mine. In a whisper he told me to hold it for him until he asked for it.

"And so," he continued, "I went down to my stateroom and called Mother to tell her about the evening, and then was awakened in the morning to the frantic screeching of Madame del Rio. And I knew that whatever had happened, I might have been able to prevent."

"Or you might have shared del Rio's fate, trying to save him," Sunday said briskly. "It would be just like you to dive in after him. Do you think a twelve-year-old boy, even you, could have changed what happened? You're being too hard on yourself."

Henry shook his head. "I suppose you're right. It's just that I keep going over and over that evening, knowing that I might have observed something untoward and not understood it at the time."

"Oh, come on, Henry," Sunday protested. "You sound like some of the people I represented as a public defender: 'The guy who shot my wife went thataway.' "

"No," Henry contradicted. "What you don't understand, darling, is that my father had told me to write down my every impression of that evening, as I had of all the other significant events at which I'd been present. My journal was a loose-leaf binder, so that in the future, I could group that chapter with others in a similar vein. Which of course is what I'm doing now that I'm writing my memoirs."

"*My* diary was in a spiral notebook," Sunday told him.

"I would very much enjoy reading it."

"Not on your life. But anyhow, what are you telling me?"

"After I spoke with Mother—even though I was extremely tired—I forced myself to make a detailed entry. I left the journal on my desk with the prime minister's envelope on top of it. During the night, those pages as well as the envelope disappeared while I slept."

Sunday looked at him, astonished.

"You mean some unknown person got into your room while you were sleeping and stole the envelope as well as your impressions of the evening?"

"Yes."

"Then, Henry dear, two words come to mind, *Foul Play.*"

* * *

"They're here, Sims," Marvin Klein called as he stood at the front windows of the salon in Belle Maris and watched the sleek yacht drop anchor.

Sims moved at a stately pace across the room where he'd been rearranging the flowers on the coffee table. "So they are," he said warmly. "And I am happy to say everything is quite in order to receive them. My, the *Columbia* is a beautiful vessel, is she not? I sailed on her several times, you know." He sighed. "Until that last dreadful event."

"You were on board the *Columbia* that night?" Marvin exclaimed.

"Yes. I had been in the employ of the family not quite two years. Mr. Henry Parker Britland the Third was kind enough to find me attentive to the small matters that make for gracious service and always took me on the yacht for special events like that weekend. The president was still just a boy, but I remember he was terribly distressed about the prime minister's disappearance. Naturally. Indeed, he was quite ill for the next several days. He had tried in his enthusiastically youthful way to determine just what *had* happened, but his father ordered the subject closed."

Sims's reflective look vanished and he allowed himself a contained smile at the sight of Henry and Sunday descending to the launch. "I am so pleased that the stone crabs are close to perfection," he told Klein. "The president will be delighted, I know."

"I'm sure he will," Marvin agreed. "But just one question, Sims. You say the subject of the prime minister's disappearance was closed. But there must have been a big investigation?"

"There was indeed, especially in view of the fact that

the prime minister's body was never found. But what could anyone say? All possible security measures had been taken. As you will see, the largest suite is a half landing above the others and has a private deck. Mr. Britland had given it to the prime minister that weekend. The minister's bodyguards were stationed at the foot of the staircase leading up to the suite. Naturally the yacht had been thoroughly searched before sailing, and everyone on board, from the crew to the personal staff, was above suspicion. The prime minister had four of his personal security guards with him as well."

"And his wife was there?"

"Yes. They were newlyweds at the time, and he never traveled without her."

"From what I understand, she became one tough cookie," Klein observed.

"Quite. She succeeded Garcia del Rio in office. Mr. Henry Parker Britland the Third never expected her to hold onto the position, but she skillfully played on the love the common people had for her late husband and eventually became entrenched. She managed to deflect much of the opposition, saying that her husband's enemies had driven him to his death. Now, of course, she is a virtual dictator."

Marvin Klein looked thoughtful. "I met her seven years ago, when President Britland had a meeting of the Central American nations. She'd just turned fifty then and was still a beauty. President Britland referred to her as 'Madame Castro.' But he would always add that if her husband hadn't died, her life would have been totally different."

Sims sighed. "Which, of course, is one of the reasons President Britland has always blamed himself. I am sure he feels that if he had accompanied the prime minister on deck that night, he might somehow have been able to prevent his death."

"I understand the prime minister had a recurring dream that he would be assassinated."

"Very Lincolnesque, wasn't it?" Sims commented. "And perhaps he anticipated his enemies by taking his own life, as the president believes. Who knows? Now, if you will excuse me, Mr. Klein, I must see to my duties. The launch bearing President and Mrs. Britland is nearing the dock."

Congor Reuthers checked into the Boca Raton Hotel, looking for all the world like a seasoned golfer out for a holiday. His light blue linen jacket hung casually over impeccably cut white jeans. A golf bag with a sufficiently used appearance was propped against his Boyd two-suiter. As a finishing touch, he had a leather camera case slung over his shoulder, but in place of a camera, it held a state-of-the-art, ultrapowerful cellular phone.

The golf bag and the handsome clubs were real but in Reuthers's hands were mere props for his pose as tourist. The clubs, in fact, had once been the property of a Costa Barria industrialist who had made the mistake of publicly criticizing Madame del Rio, and had been left behind with virtually all his other worldly possessions when he made his escape from the island.

Reuthers realized suddenly that the clerk was speaking to him. What was the fellow blathering about? he asked himself irritably. Something about golf.

"Yes, yes," he said quickly. "I'm looking forward to a few innings of golf. Love the game, you know."

Unaware of his gaffe, he turned imperiously and followed the bellman to the suite from which he intended to direct his mandated operation, the search of the *Columbia*.

At four o'clock the phone rang.

The caller was Lenny Wallace, also known as Len Pagan, but whose real name was Lorenzo Esperanza, the mole Reuthers had managed to place on the crew of the *Columbia*.

With satisfaction, Reuthers called to mind the man's baby face, complete with angelic smile, fuzz on the upper lip, freckles across the bridge of the nose, and big ears. Len resembled nothing so much as a young Mickey Rooney as he had looked in his long-ago movie role as Andy Hardy.

In truth, he was a cold-blooded killer.

"It's not going to be easy," Len drawled.

Reuthers bit his lip, reminding himself that this insolent hatchet man was a special favorite of Prime Minister Angelica del Rio. Then he reminded himself that she always could be counted upon to punish failure. "Why ever not?" he snapped.

"Because President Britland's wife is nosy, always snooping around. And also she is asking a lot of questions about that night."

Reuthers felt his palms begin to sweat. "Like what?"

"I pretended to be polishing something in the dining room when she and Britland were there. I overheard them talking about the dinner with del Rio; she was asking him where everyone sat."

"He was only twelve years old at the time," Reuthers protested. "What could he possibly remember that would make a difference to us now?"

"She said something like she'd never heard him, I mean

her husband, talk so much about having been tired. She said something like, 'You were *tired*, the prime minister was *tired*, your father was *tired*. What did you people have for dessert that night, Valium?' "

Reuthers closed his eyes, ignoring the splendid sight of the sun beginning its majestic descent. His worst nightmare had just come true. They were getting too close for comfort. "You've got to find those papers," he ordered.

"Look, the place is swarming with Secret Service. I'll get one chance and one chance only, so your information had better be right. You're sure you hid the papers in Stateroom A?"

"You insolent thug, of *course* I'm sure," Reuthers snapped.

The memory of that night made him shiver. After he had gone through the prime minister's jacket, he had realized that the envelope was gone. *I knew the boy was the last one to talk to him. I knew he must have slipped the envelope to him. I had to find his stateroom in the pitch dark. The kid was in Stateroom A. With my lousy sense of direction, I opened the wrong door. Suppose someone had been in Stateroom B.*

Reuthers still got cold sweats remembering how he had tiptoed into the boy's cabin, praying that the steward wouldn't come back, find the corridor light out, and investigate. Then, armed with a pencil-beam flashlight, he had made his way to the desk and picked up del Rio's envelope. By a stroke of luck he happened to glance at the open journal. Realizing what it contained as he read it, he tore the last entry from the binder.

But then he had heard the handle of the door turning and the boy began to stir. Quickly he had hidden in the closet. Feeling trapped, he had searched in the dark for any possible way out. Instead, he found a hole cut in the wall. Fearing that he might be discovered and searched, he had shoved the journal pages and del Rio's envelope into the opening.

From inside the closet he had listened as someone came in, walked over to the bed, then turned and left. When he went to retrieve the papers, however, he couldn't reach them. For nearly an hour he had struggled to get his hand down, feeling his fingers on the tip of the envelope and not able to grasp it. Then, on cue, Madame del Rio sounded the alarm. *I barely got out of the room before the kid woke up,* he remembered. *She shrieked like a banshee.* He learned that the next day safes were installed in all the staterooms. That was why the hole had been prepared in the closet wall.

"This is gonna be a tough one," Len was saying. "Britland's Secret Service guys are smart. Eyes in the back of the head, that kind of thing. The top one already yelled at me for going into the dining room when the Britlands were there."

"That is not my concern!" Reuthers snapped. "Let me put it this way. If you can retrieve those papers safely and get away, you'll enjoy the grateful thanks of a powerful boss. If you mess this up, your aging mother and her eight sisters will be dispatched to the hereafter."

Len's voice became pleading. "I love my Mama and my aunties."

"Then I would suggest you get those papers back, no matter *what* you have to do. Do you understand? That hole was in the wall because a safe was being installed the next day. The scheduled renovation may expose them. Break through the paneling at the rear of the closet of Stateroom A. *They're in there!* I don't care how you do it, just do it, and don't make any mistakes."

"Henry, when you told your father about the missing papers, what did he *do?*" Sunday asked as she sipped champagne in the glassed-in salon of the *Columbia*. A semicircular room at the back of the ship, the salon seated about ten people comfortably, and as Henry had explained, it was a location preferred by many dignitaries for conversation, reading, or simply observing the horizon.

"I'm afraid that with the calamity of the prime minister's disappearance, Father was not too impressed by my tale of missing papers. The prime minister had a habit of doodling on dinner menus or printed speeches, and I know Father thought that possibly he had passed something of the sort to me as a joke."

"What about your journal entry?"

"He told me to rewrite it when I felt better. I had awakened with a headache, some sort of bug, I assume, and of course all hell was breaking loose. Helicopters were swarming around looking for any sign of the body. Boats, Navy divers, you name it."

"Do you believe that del Rio gave you some sort of doodle in that envelope?"

"No, I don't."

"Was a search made for your missing papers?"

"In fairness to Father, yes, there was. At his instructions, Sims personally went through my stateroom to be sure I hadn't been mistaken about leaving the envelope with the journal on the desk. But he found nothing."

"And of course since you'd written in a loose-leaf

binder, it wasn't as though you could show pages had been *ripped* from your journal."

"Exactly." He paused and looked at his wife, his affection for her obvious in his eyes. He smiled, then said, "Incidentally, if your constituents could see you now, they'd never vote for you. You look about twelve years old."

Sunday was wearing a long, wraparound flowered skirt, a sleeveless white tee shirt, and sandals. She raised an eyebrow. "At this moment I may not look like a member of Congress," she said with dignity, "but for your information all these questions are not caused by idle, childish curiosity, or even, darling, because I know how troubled you are about that night. I feel exactly the same as you do about Madame del Rio. I'd like to see Costa Barria have a crack at a fair, nonoppressive government. But it would take a lot to get the people so riled up that they would take action against her, and unless something dramatic happens, she's going to breeze through that election. It's as good as fixed."

"Yes, she is."

"And it maddens me to think that one of Garcia del Rio's group may have stolen his suicide note, if that's what it was, from your room while you slept. There's no way of knowing, but it *could* have made a difference."

"It maddens me even more to think that I might have saved the prime minister's life if I had strolled the deck with him. That's really why I bought the *Columbia*. Except for that incident it has such a great and distinguished history. I want to remove the taint somehow."

Sims quietly entered the room carrying a tray of cheese

puffs. He offered it to Sunday. As she accepted one, she said to him, "Sims, you were on this yacht before?"

"Yes, madam."

"How does it look to you?"

Sims's forehead crinkled. "Very well kept indeed, madam, but if I may observe, it is rather shocking that absolutely nothing has changed. By that I mean the wall coverings, the bedding, the upholstery, the draperies. During the thirty-two years the *Columbia* was in the possession of Mr. Hodgins Weatherby, he clearly treated it rather as a shrine."

Henry chuckled. "I can explain that: Weatherby was no sailor. In fact, the sight of a lapping wave was torture to him. He paid a fortune to dredge the harbor so he could walk aboard from the dock, and other than maintenance people, no one was allowed aboard except him and his psychic. He'd always sit here"—Henry patted the arm of the chair in which he was seated, then pointed to the one where Sunday was perched—"and the psychic, there.

"I didn't tell you, darling, but you're in Sir Winston Churchill's seat. From what Father told me, when FDR borrowed the yacht from my father to take Churchill for a sail, he made a beeline for that seat. Through the psychic, old Weatherby claimed to have held conversations with the prime minister, as well as with FDR, de Gaulle, and Eisenhower, to name but a few. I understand, however, that he wouldn't exchange a word with Stalin."

"He treated the boat as nothing more than an exotic gazebo," Sunday said. "I can understand why Weatherby's family was ready to donate her to the charity auction when he died."

"I can too. But of course that's what gave rise to the

idea of the ship's being haunted. Apparently the psychic was a pretty good mimic."

There was a tap on the door. Marvin Klein came in hesitantly. "Mr. President, I tried not to interrupt, but the secretary of state is calling."

"Tony?" Henry said. "Something must be up." He took the phone from Klein's hand, then hissed, "Sims, don't go away. Give me some of those cheese puffs."

He swallowed one quickly, then spoke heartily into the phone. "Hello, Tony. Ranger keeping you busy, I hope?"

Ranger was the Secret Service code name for the chief executive.

Secretary of State Anthony Pryor had been tapped for the top cabinet position by Henry's successor, President Desmond Ogilvey. A friend of Henry's since their Harvard days, Pryor delighted in dropping his formal demeanor when talking to him. "Henry, I'm busier than a fox in a chicken coop," he said, "but you know that. Look, you bought the *Columbia* back, and now we're hoping that you'll help us out with something. You're going to get a call from Miguel Alesso's people. He wants to see you. Ranger wants you to see him."

"Alesso? He's running against the prime minister of Costa Barria."

"You bet he is. And he's in Miami incognito. He swears that Angelica del Rio engineered her husband's murder thirty-two years ago, and that her agents were trying to buy the *Columbia* at the auction, only you beat them to it."

"How does he know that?" Henry asked quietly.

"Because the widow of one of the guys who screwed up the purchase last week called him. The point is, Ranger figures that you of all people would be able to spot holes in Alesso's story. If you think it holds water, it says a lot about what our position should be on that coming election. Even though thirty-two years have passed Garcia del Rio is considered practically a saint in his country. Don't forget Angelica del Rio is scheduled to come here on a state visit in exchange for guaranteeing human rights and releasing dissidents. Ranger doesn't want to end up with egg on his face if someone proves she masterminded her husband's murder."

"You mean Des thinks this may be a tactic to prevent Prime Minister del Rio from getting our approval just before the election?"

"You got it. God, Henry, these damned small countries can drive you nuts, can't they?"

"No more than the big ones," Henry reminded him. "Of course I'll see Alesso. Tomorrow morning, here on the *Columbia.*"

"Great. We'll make all the arrangements."

Henry handed the phone back to Marvin Klein and looked at Sunday. "My dear," he said, "it may be that as usual you were right."

"About what?"

"About Garcia del Rio's death."

Congor Reuthers had learned long ago that even a man under the gun needs nourishment. This was Monday. Lenny had gotten word to him that the Britlands were scheduled to fly to Washington Wednesday morning, when Congresswoman Sandra O'Brien Britland needed to be on Capitol Hill for the final debate on aid to Costa Barria. Once the Britlands were off the boat, all extra crew members, including Lenny, would be discharged. Which meant that they were running out of time. Lenny had to get into Stateroom A tomorrow.

For the moment, however, there was nothing more that Reuthers could do. Except eat. Having become particularly fond of the ambiance of the tower restaurant of the Boca Raton Hotel, he decided to head there. Surely a few martinis and a lobster would refresh his spirits. Reaching for the phone, he dialed the tower and imperiously ordered a window table, one facing the inland waterway.

When he arrived at the maître d's desk, he was outraged to find that he could not have his table of choice. Forced to decide whether to stomp out or to accept fate, he allowed his stomach to make the decision.

"I am sure you will understand why we had to rearrange our seatings, sir," the maitre d' said with a nervous smirk as he led Reuthers to a table where the only nearby sign of water was in a pitcher. "You see why we had to keep some tables clear," he whispered, gesturing to the wall of windows.

Reuthers's heart leaped. Seated by themselves, chatting over cocktails, tanned and smiling, were America's favorite couple, the former president of the United States and his congresswoman bride.

Reuthers reached into his pocket for the cigarette case that concealed his eavesdropping device. Casually he placed it open on the table and pointed it in the direction of the Britlands. As though scratching his head, he inserted the tiny receiver in his ear and was rewarded by hearing Henry Parker Britland IV say, "I'll be interested in meeting with Alesso tomorrow."

Alesso! Reuthers thought. *Alesso!* Why would Britland be meeting with him?

He cupped his ear to block out the hum from surrounding tables, then realized he was being addressed.

"I'm sorry, sir, this is a smoke-free environment." Reuthers looked up to see the disapproving frown on the face of the dining-room captain and realized he had missed something Sunday Britland had said about "Alesso bringing proof . . ."

"I am *not* smoking," Reuthers contradicted. Pointedly the captain looked at the open cigarette case.

"I keep it out only to test my willpower," Reuthers snapped.

"Then, sir, with your permission." The captain moved the case so that it was almost concealed between the bud vase and the basket of bread a busboy had just placed on the table. "Now you can peek at it, but other diners won't see it and have the impression that this is a smoking area. Remember, you may not be the only one here resisting temptation. Oh my, wouldn't that be a can of worms? Sir, have you ever thought to reduce your craving for nicotine by chewing gum? It does help."

"Get out of there, you fool. Britland is looking at you."

Reuthers jumped as a familiar voice seared his eardrum with acidic anger.

"He might recognize you, you imbecile."

Reuthers looked around, his eyes wildly searching the room. What disguise was Angelica assuming today? She had to be frantic with worry if she had come here instead of going directly to Costa Barria from New York. He spotted a gray-haired solitary diner, one elbow on the table, staring at her wineglass. There she was, Lonesome Wilma, another of Angelica's personas. His searching glance next went over to a window table where it locked with the intense gaze of the former president of the United States. It had been thirty-two years since they had met. Reuthers had been on the fateful trip, ostensibly as one of Garcia del Rio's personal bodyguards and, theoretically, had been executed with the rest of his staff for dereliction of duty in failing to protect the prime minister.

Could Britland recognize him after all these years?

Afraid to risk the possibility of discovery, Reuthers jumped up and turned his back on the former president. "I do not choose to dine here," he barked, and hurried from the dining room.

He was at the elevator when the captain caught up with him. "You forgot your cigarette case, sir," he said. "Keep up the good work in resisting temptation. Courage!"

Senior Secret Service agent Jack Collins stirred restlessly. He was seated a table away from former President Britland, and that inner voice which warned him of danger was shrieking at him now.

Something was up. His eyes moved restlessly around the room, scanning the occupants with MRI intensity. The diners were obviously affluent—a lot of older couples, some family groups with young children. They were all tanned, relaxed, and smiling. A group of suits were swapping stories.

Probably here on a golf outing that would be charged to their company as a business meeting, Collins thought sourly.

He watched as a ramrod-postured male, every inch of his body showing annoyance, exited the restaurant, almost colliding with four well-dressed women in their sixties. Collins observed the ladies follow the maître d' into the room, then register obvious displeasure when he escorted them to a back table situated between the family groups. If they had a man with them that wouldn't happen, he thought.

He noticed a woman at the smallest window table, looking pensively out over the water. Gray hair, a lined face, plain sunglasses, a woebegone expression—she looked like someone recently bereaved.

Collins's eyes moved past her, on down the row of tables. He just didn't like the vibes he was getting. Something seemed wrong here. It was a distinct relief when, an hour later, the Britlands got up to go.

As they passed the reservations desk, the former president beckoned to Collins. "Jack," he said, "a guy in the dining room left abruptly without eating. Did you notice him? There was something familiar about him. See what you can find out."

Collins nodded. Signaling the four accompanying agents to close around the Britlands, he sent them ahead, while he stopped at the desk.

When he returned to Belle Maris an hour later, he had already arranged for round-the-clock surveillance of the hotel guest registered under the name of "Norman Ballinger." The dining-room captain's tale of the open cigarette case, followed by the room clerk's amused description of Ballinger's plans to have "innings of golf" —no wonder his instincts were on red alert, he thought.

His beeper sounded seconds after he entered the mansion. "You're onto something, Jack," headquarters informed him. "Ballinger is really Congor Reuthers, the one person close to Angelica del Rio. He's always in the background of the political scene, but the word is that he has stayed in favor by being her troubleshooter."

"What's he doing in Boca Raton?" Collins demanded.

"We think he knows Alesso is there and wants to keep track of his movements. We'll have him tailed, but be on guard. Reuthers doesn't get his own hands dirty. He may have others with him."

Collins got off the phone and wished he could shake the ominous feeling that Henry Parker Britland IV should not have purchased the *Columbia*.

On Tuesday morning, Lenny Wallace was painfully aware of the heightened security on the *Columbia*.

At 7 A.M. he had checked in with Reuthers and had been informed that Miguel Alesso, the dissident leader running against the prime minister in next week's election, was to have lunch with former President Britland on the yacht.

"You must retrieve those papers," Reuthers had snapped at him. "The prime minister is *personally* involved in this. Failure is not an option."

He then instructed Lenny to find some way to get into the dining room so that he could try to overhear what was being said at the luncheon.

Lenny made a supreme effort to keep from telling Reuthers that only an imbecile would believe that a deckhand, unless he were invisible, could wander into any room where a highly confidential top-level meeting was taking place. Instead, he thought of Mama and his aunties and promised to do his very best.

He *did* point out that when the former president was aboard the *Columbia*, his senior Secret Service agent, Jack

Collins, was also there, and seemed to have the ability to know any time anyone on the boat so much as sneezed.

Reuthers had one last word: "You should know that your mother and her sisters are under house arrest—only temporarily, I'm sure. Do whatever you think best."

At precisely twelve o'clock, Lenny was on the crew deck, binoculars pressed to his eyes, observing as a limo pulled up to the dock. He watched as two men and a woman stepped from it and boarded the launch: the Britlands, and with them, the opposition leader of Costa Barria, Miguel Alesso.

An unexplored possibility crossed Lenny's mind: Alesso was gaining in popularity. Everywhere he made an appearance, the people went wild. *Suppose I can't find the papers? I could just disappear. If by some crazy chance he wins the election, I could get in touch with him, tell him what I was assigned to do. Then I could tell him where the bodies are buried. Maybe he'd reward me.*

But no, that could not be. He knew that. By the time the election was over it would be too late for his Mama and his aunties, those wonderful women who were known as the "Alphabet Sisters." Mama, the oldest, was Antonella, the next oldest was Bianca, the third, Concetta, and so on until the youngest, Iona.

Lorenzo Esperanza, aka Lenny Wallace, felt a renewed sense of duty as he brushed the tears from his eyes.

The ring of truth, Sunday thought. *It emanates from him.* She and Henry were seated with Miguel Alesso in the salon. Henry had suggested that Alesso take Sir Winston's favorite armchair.

"I'm out of my league," Alesso said with a slight smile,

"although in a small way I may be able to compare my country's precarious state with that of England during World War II."

Sunday knew that Alesso was scarcely thirty years old, but his air of grave maturity, his dark hair, heavily streaked with gray, and the wise yet sad expression in his hazel eyes combined to make him seem at least a decade older.

Now he leaned forward, his demeanor intense. "Angelica del Rio planned and carried out the assassination of a truly great man," he said passionately. "Her father, as you know, sir, was the commander of Costa Barria's army. She married the prime minister on her father's orders, always —I am convinced—with the intention of eliminating him. She was then and remains now a great beauty and also quite charismatic. And after all, as the saying goes, a man is a man . . ."

He shrugged mournfully. "She changed his personal bodyguards, replaced them with the thugs who betrayed him, including her distant English cousin, who is now known as Congor Reuthers.

"According to information I have gathered, she drugged her husband as well as your father and yourself, sir, with the special dessert her personal chef prepared. It was she who rendered Garcia del Rio unconscious. His bodyguards, led by Reuthers, weighted down his body and threw it overboard. It must have sunk to the very bottom of the ocean.

"The bodyguards expected to be rewarded. They were. Upon their return to Costa Barria with the grieving widow, they were executed for dereliction of duty—all except, of course, for Reuthers."

"I still don't understand why she chose *that* night, on *this* yacht," Henry observed.

Sunday studied her husband. He sat erect in his captain's chair, his chin resting on his left hand, his entire being concentrated on Alesso. She could almost hear the strains of "Hail to the Chief" floating through the air.

"Angelica had received a phone call from her father, the general, telling her that her husband was aware of an impending assassination attempt involving his bodyguards. He also informed her that del Rio was aware of the millions of dollars she had siphoned from the charities she headed. He was planning to have her arrested when they returned to Costa Barria. There was no other option. She had to make her move immediately."

Makes sense, Sunday agreed silently.

"Their plan was that Angelica's father would take over the government. But the general suffered a heart attack the next week, and she seized the opportunity to take over herself. She filled out her husband's term of office, then, capitalizing on the love the people had for him, she seized absolute power."

"What proof is there of all this?" Henry asked. "You did talk about proof, señor."

Alesso shrugged. "The proof is in the envelope that Garcia del Rio passed to you when you were a twelve-year-old boy."

"And how do you know all this?" the former president asked.

"One of the bodyguards tried to bribe a prison official to allow him to escape execution," Alesso replied. "He told the official about del Rio's murder and said that Reuthers had searched del Rio's body for an envelope before it was thrown overboard. The envelope contained a statement from del Rio, the one he was planning to make, accusing his wife. She had managed to get a glimpse of it, but didn't have time to remove it from his jacket before they went to dinner."

"Why didn't any of this ever come out?" Sunday asked.

Alesso looked astonished at the question. "The prison official would have signed his own death warrant if he had admitted he knew the prime minister had been murdered," he said. "But as he got older and drank a little more wine, as old men sometimes do, he began to talk. Eventually he talked too much. Then he disappeared."

"And now, all these years later, the puzzle is finally put together," Henry mused.

"No, sir," Alesso corrected, "the puzzle is not together until those papers, if they still exist, are located. But for the immediate present, I beg both of you to support my candidacy. I beg you, Congresswoman Britland, not to vote aid to my people while Angelica del Rio remains in power. To support her is to support oppression."

Sunday found herself unable to hold his intense gaze. She looked away, afraid to let him see the indecision in her own eyes.

"And you, sir," Alesso said, looking at Henry, "I implore you to urge the chief executive of the United States to cancel any plans to honor Angelica del Rio with a state dinner. The imprimatur of your great nation must not be given to strengthen a tyrant's hand."

Lenny knew there was no way he could hope to get on the upper deck while the meeting was taking place. But he did learn that after the luncheon the Britlands were returning to Belle Maris until their early-morning departure for Washington. That meant the omnipresent Secret Service would be guarding the mansion, not the yacht.

Lenny was scheduled to go off duty at 5 P.M. He knew it would seem odd if he did not make an immediate beeline for shore. As he scrubbed the teak deck, he hit upon an idea. No one would expect someone with food poisoning to leave his bunk.

An hour later he presented himself to the purser. Perspirationlike moisture covered his face, his eyelids were at half-mast, his gait unsteady.

"Something I ate," he whined, clutching at his stomach.

Ten minutes later he was in his cabin on the crew deck, lying on his bunk and getting up his courage to sneak up to Stateroom A. That would have to wait until later, though, under the cover of late-night darkness and lightened security.

"Coming events cast their shadows before," Henry thought that evening as he sipped espresso.

He and Sunday were dining on the flower-filled terrace of Belle Maris. Tapered candles sent soft, flickering points of flame toward the full moon, which bathed the *Columbia* in eerie majesty.

"Darling, you're so quiet," Sunday observed as she nodded to Sims to accept a refill of her double espresso.

"Even you won't sleep after all that coffee," Henry admonished mildly.

"You know me, Henry. I could sack out on a picket fence. It's my clear conscience that does the trick." She took a sip and smacked her lips. "As the old saying went, 'Man, that's coffee.'"

Her expression became serious. "Henry, I haven't asked

you yet, but I'm going to now. You *do* believe Alesso's story, don't you?"

"Yes, I do, for more than one reason. Last night at the restaurant I got a good look at that man who seemed so familiar. As you know, I was right. I *had* seen him before. He's Angelica del Rio's right-hand man. And he was on the *Columbia* that night thirty-two years ago. He was near the prime minister and me when del Rio passed me the envelope. Logically, when he didn't find it on del Rio, he'd suspect I had it. If he knows Alesso has uncovered the truth, he'll move heaven and earth to get that envelope back. If I could take the yacht apart inch by inch, I would. But it was out of our hands for thirty-two years. Who knows if some maid didn't find it stuck somewhere and just toss it out!"

"Are you going to suggest that Des cancel the state visit for Madame del Rio?" Sunday asked.

"State visits aren't easily canceled, darling, except for grave reasons. If Madame del Rio wins the election next Tuesday and signs the human-rights agreement, stories circulated by her defeated opponent will be discounted. Without proof they simply cannot be considered credible. And as of now, Alesso has zero chance to beat her."

Sunday stared out at the *Columbia*. "Henry, know what? I'd like to spend one more night on the yacht. I love sleeping there. Would you mind?"

Henry smiled. "I'm assuming I'm included in the plan. I think I would enjoy being rocked by the ocean myself, my love. Of course we'll go. Who knows, maybe the *Columbia* will give up her secrets to us. Wouldn't that be a cause to rejoice?"

* * *

At nine o'clock, before he left his cabin to retrieve the missing papers, Lenny arranged his bunk to give the appearance of a sleeping form within it.

He had observed many cutters surrounding the *Columbia* and gleefully reminded himself that while they could make sure no one got *on* it, *he* was already there!

Now that it was time to do the job, his nerves were tingling. The danger was in getting to Stateroom A. Once inside, he should be home free. There was no reason for *anyone* to even glance into the stateroom tonight.

The hardest part would be to cut out a section of the thick oak paneling without making a noise. Reuthers had said that the envelope and journal pages had been dropped into the hole created for the safe, so they couldn't have fallen any farther than to the floor, and he should find them there, behind the paneling.

So it made sense to start at the *bottom,* he reasoned. It would be easier to reach up than down if the papers were wedged inside the wall.

Armed with a saw, a small hammer, and a drill he had stolen from the equipment room, he cautiously left the crew's quarters.

The first two decks were clear. Obviously any guards were on the dock or in boats. On the upper deck he barely avoided walking into a Secret Service man stationed at the staircase that led to the private suite the Britlands used.

Waste of manpower, Lenny thought, since they're staying at the house. But the near miss worried him. They *were* staying in the house, weren't they? he wondered.

Three harrowing minutes later, he slipped into Stateroom A. He didn't dare turn on the light, but fortunately the night was clear and the full moon illuminated everything. The stateroom was twenty times the size of the cubicle they had given him; it had a double bed with headboard, a built-in desk, built-in dressers, a sofa and chairs—everything to assure that even in a rough sea the occupant wouldn't be inconvenienced.

The closet was deep. Once inside, Lenny closed the door; only then did he feel able to turn on the flashlight in safety. There it was against the back wall, the safe! Round in shape to resemble a port hole, its door painted to depict a tranquil sea, the old-fashioned combination lock made to resemble a compass, it commanded Lenny's undivided attention.

He ran his fingers over it, reflecting that no gem that ever would be locked *in* it would be half so valuable as what was hidden *under* it.

He sat on the floor and tapped the wood paneling to measure its thickness. Thick, he told himself, damn thick! A lot of trees bit the dust to build this boat, he thought, as he anticipated a long night's work. Sure, if he had a big ax and an electric saw—and wanted to attract every guard and crew member aboard—he could make fast work of it, but that wasn't in the cards. Cautiously he began to drill a hole a few inches up from the flooring.

Every fifteen minutes he paused to rest. Nearly two hours later, as he was stretching, he thought he heard a faint click. Snapping off the flashlight, he opened the closet door a crack. His eyes bulged in alarm.

Standing in the quiet room, her back to him, a single desk lamp illuminating her slender nightgown-clad body, Congresswoman Sandra O'Brien Britland was turning down the covers. As Lenny watched in disbelief, she got into bed and turned off the light.

* * *

As usual, Henry is right, Sunday thought with a sigh, as she tried to settle down, having left her husband fast asleep in their suite on the deck above. *Too much coffee.* Her brain was racing. But it wasn't just the coffee. There was something Henry had told her about that night he had spent in this very cabin thirty-two years ago that was hammering at her subconscious. What was it?

If only those papers could be found, she thought. If Alesso is right, a woman murdered her husband on this yacht and the proof may have been stolen from the desk in this room.

Clearly, sleep was out of the question. Henry was usually the one to read for several hours after she dropped off, but tonight he had dropped into a heavy slumber the moment his head hit the pillow.

It happened so seldom that she had decided to tiptoe into the sitting room of the suite rather than to lie there stirring about and risk disturbing him. But then the idea of coming down to this cabin had hit her. After all, this was where the theft took place.

Henry had told her something important about what had taken place in this room the night del Rio disappeared. But what? It must be something seemingly *trivial* that everyone had missed.

She had reasoned that if she came to the cabin where whatever it was had occurred, that might help to bring elusive facts to the surface. Before leaving the suite, she had scrawled a note to Henry and left it on the pillow. He worries too much about me, she had thought as she placed it there, resisting the impulse to draw up the coverlet around his neck. It might only awaken him. And he might not want her to go.

Art, the Secret Service agent stationed at the foot of the staircase, had been surprised to see her but had nodded when she told him where she would be.

I hope he doesn't think Henry and I had an argument, she'd thought, amused at the notion that they could ever argue. We just debate things every now and then, that's all. Intellectual discussions, she reasoned. But certainly not arguments.

Giving up on sleep, Sunday reached over and turned the light back on. Sitting up, she brushed her hair away from her face and plumped the pillows behind her. Sims had said that the ship's furnishings hadn't been changed. She imagined Henry sitting at the desk, writing a detailed entry even though, as he had told her, he was so tired he could hardly keep his eyes open.

I wonder if when you're very tired, you don't almost spirit-write instead of consciously thinking, Sunday considered. Oh well, she thought, sighing, this isn't getting me anywhere. I'd better try again to get to sleep.

She turned off the light again. It was so quiet!

Henry told me he has not so much memories of that night as he does impressions. Of someone in the room, and of someone standing over him. We *do* know his father looked in on him. But could there have been someone else? she wondered.

What else did he tell me that I can't recall? Why do I have a creepy feeling about all this?

The quiet was broken by a slight creak as the tempo of the boat's rocking began to increase. Another creak followed, this one less general, and much closer. Sunday's head turned instinctively toward the closet wall.

She had heard a sound, like something sliding along the

floor. And it seemed to be coming from inside the closet. It sounded as if someone were in there. She was *sure* of it.

Cautiously she slid her hand along the night table, searching for the button that would summon help, but as she did, the door from the corridor opened, the light went on, and she looked into her husband's concerned eyes.

Whoever is in that closet obviously didn't expect me, she thought. *He's looking for something.*

"*Sunday!*" Henry exclaimed. "Whatever possessed you to . . . ?"

"Oh, sweetheart," she interrupted, her voice above normal pitch. "I'm ready to go back up now. I can't seem to get to sleep here, either."

"I warned you about the coffee," Henry admonished.

"I know, darling, you're always right. That's why they elected you president."

Sunday hopped out of bed, grabbed her robe, and almost shoved Henry out the door, pulling it closed behind them with a decisive click.

In the corridor, she put her hand over his mouth just as he started to ask what on earth was going on.

"I've cornered our man," she whispered fiercely. "He's in there, in the closet. I'd just realized it when you came in. Ten to one he's looking for the papers that disappeared that night, and he must know they're somewhere in the closet. We'll let him find them for us."

An hour later, Lenny was still sawing away at an ever-widening hole in the back wall of the closet of Stateroom A. Reuthers must have been dreaming, he thought, growing increasingly frustrated and on the verge of becoming frantic. Those papers aren't here. They're just not here!

Mama! My aunties! Tia Bianca, Tia Concetta, Tia Desdemona, Tia Eugenia, Tia Florina, Tia Georgina, Tia Helena, Tia Iona . . .

Tears of frustration began to roll down Lenny's cheeks. The papers weren't here, and he would be blamed. He would have to figure out some way to save everyone's neck, his included, but for now he had to get back to his bunk. There was no telling if someone might not wander into the cabin again.

He left the closet, closing the door securely behind him; he tiptoed across the room to the outer door and opened it cautiously. Then he froze.

He was looking into the steely eyes of senior Secret Service agent Jack Collins.

"Show us the buried treasure," Collins ordered as other agents grabbed Lenny's arms.

At Collins's insistence, Henry and Sunday were at the end of the corridor, separated from the action by four burly agents. When he signaled, one of them said to the former president, "If you wish, sir . . ." and stepped aside.

Collins pushed Lenny back into the stateroom. "Obviously, he was looking for something, sir," he said, pointing to the destroyed back wall of the closet. "He's one of the deckhands. A deplorable lapse of security."

"Never mind that," Henry interrupted. "Did he find the missing papers?"

"There are no papers on him, sir."

Lenny knew his only hope was to cut a deal, and fast. "I'll tell you anything," he implored, "but if I do, can you stop them from hurting Mama and my aunties?"

"We can try," Henry promised. "Talk!"

"Mr. President, your bathrobe, sir," said Sims, who had appeared in the doorway.

The man even looks dignified with his nightshirt on, Sunday thought. Sims had arrived wearing a morning coat over the nightshirt, black silk socks and black oxfords.

"Just a minute, Sims." Henry went eye to eye with Lenny. "I said, Talk."

". . . and so Reuthers knows that you're taking the boat apart to renovate it. He knows that if *you* found the envelope and your journal pages from that night, it would be all over for Angelica del Rio. The people would lynch her. He said the papers would be behind the closet wall under the safe, but he's wrong. The papers must have evaporated. They just aren't there."

Sunday saw her own leaden disappointment reflected in her husband's face.

"Your bathrobe, sir," Sims urged. "You'll catch your death of cold. He shivered suddenly. "Oh dear! Déjà vu! This reminds me of that dreadful night thirty-two years ago. After the prime minister's disappearance, I brought you your bathrobe and escorted you to your father's suite . . ."

"Wait a minute!" Sunday exclaimed. "What did you just say?"

"I said I brought Mr. Henry—that's what I called him in those days—his robe and then—"

"That's what I mean," Sunday said. "You *brought* him his robe. Why wasn't it in his stateroom?"

Sims's brow furrowed, then cleared.

"Of course. Of *course*. That's how it happened. I had personally brought up your milk and cookies, sir, and checked to be sure all was in readiness. I noted a most annoying dripping sound coming from the water closet in Stateroom A and decided to put you in Stateroom B for the night."

Sims frowned thoughtfully. "Yes, I remember clearly. I brought your pajamas into Stateroom B, I turned down the bed. I transferred your milk and cookies. Knowing you would wish to write in your journal, I also moved your journal and pen onto the desk in B."

"Of course!" Henry exclaimed. "The door was open, you were here, and I was so groggy I didn't even notice that I was going into Stateroom B."

Sunday turned to Jack Collins. "Jack, let's take an ax to the closet wall next door."

Fifteen minutes later, the former president of the United States looked up from the yellowing pages he had just read. "It's all here," he said emotionally. "Jack, get me the special phone. I need to talk to President Ogilvey immediately."

Three minutes later, Henry was on the phone to his successor in the Oval Office, reading him the last written words of Garcia del Rio:

"It is with heavy heart that I order the arrest of my wife, Señora Angelica del Rio, and of her father, Generalissimo José Imperate, on the charges of treason and grand larceny.

"I have learned that an attempt is to be made on my life next Tuesday. The informant is uncertain if it is to take place when I am driven from the palace to address our congress or later at the private dinner that

I will host for my party leaders. The new chef that my wife chose may be planning to poison all of us. I believe that my wife and her father have ensured my lack of protection by having trumped-up charges placed against the good and honest men who have guarded me for years. They have replaced them with their own henchmen, led by a man I now know to be Angelica's distant cousin, one Congor Reuthers, who was raised in England.

"In a separate charge I accuse my wife of the crime of grand larceny. She has stolen millions of dollars from the charitable foundations she heads, dollars that were given and intended for the destitute of our country. In support of that charge I herewith list her numbered accounts in Switzerland.

"That's it, Des," Henry concluded. "My journal entry notes that when my father stood up to speak at dinner, Garcia del Rio surreptitiously changed his plate for his wife's. My guess is that even though he didn't expect to be poisoned that night, he was always on guard. Then I made an observation about the crème brûlée her personal chef, whom she had insisted accompany her, had prepared —that it tasted faintly medicinal to me. I think we were all drugged with a sedative to be sure that no one would be able to come to del Rio's aid. I noted that she never touched the dessert. But that at her insistence he sampled hers."

Henry paused and sighed. "Obviously he was overpowered even though he ate very little of it. And now, my friend, the ball's in your court."

He handed the phone to Jack Collins and turned to Sunday. "It's over, darling."

"It's really quite wonderful, isn't it?" Sunday asked emotionally as, a week later, she and Henry watched the newly elected prime minister, Miguel Alesso, wave to the cheering multitudes in Costa Barria.

"He'll make a fine leader," Henry agreed. "And he'll bring to fruition the dream Garcia del Rio had for his country—human rights, a democratic government, a sound economy, educational opportunities."

They were in the library at Drumdoe, watching the special election report that had followed the eleven o'clock news.

Sunday reached for Henry's hand. "You are convinced now that you couldn't have changed what happened even if you had walked on the deck with del Rio that night?"

"Yes, I'm convinced," Henry agreed. "I'm only grateful that at that last moment some impulse made him slip that envelope into my pocket. Otherwise we'd never have known."

"And at least Angelica and her cousin will pay for their crimes," Sunday said. "I don't think that lady will enjoy life imprisonment."

"I'm sure she won't." Henry smiled. "Shall we have one more sail on the *Columbia* before the renovating starts?"

"I'd like that," Sunday agreed.

"But this time try to stay in the stateroom with me. I don't like looking for you in the middle of the night."

"I'll stay put. You never know who you'll find in a closet on that yacht, do you?" Sunday asked, with a smile.

Merry
Christmas /
Joyeux Noël

◆

> "Heap on more wood!—the wind is chill;
> But let it whistle as it will,
> We'll keep our Christmas merry still."

Congresswoman Sandra O'Brien Britland looked up to see her poetry-spouting husband, the former president of the United States, standing in the doorway of her cozy office in Drumdoe, their country home in Bernardsville, New Jersey.

She smiled affectionately. Even in a turtleneck sweater, jeans, and worn ankle boots, Henry Parker Britland IV exuded a natural born-to-the-manner persona. The touches of gray in his dark brown hair, and thoughtful creases in his forehead, were almost the only signs that Henry was approaching his forty-fifth birthday.

"So it's Tennyson we're quoting," she said as she uncurled herself from the couch where she had been reading the seemingly endless stack of material about pending legislation. "I gather the 'All-Around Hunk' is up to something."

"Not Tennyson, love. Sir Walter Scott, and be aware I will hang you by the thumbs if you call me 'All-Around Hunk' again."

"But *People* magazine just voted you that for the fifth year in a row. That's a real record. Pretty soon they'll have to create a 'Perennial Hunk' award and retire you from active consideration."

Seeing the mock-menacing look on Henry's face, Sunday said hastily, "Okay, okay. Just kidding."

"Your saw, Mr. President." Sims, the butler, appeared in the doorway, carrying a shiny new saw across upturned palms. He displayed it to Henry with the same reverence he might have shown in tendering the crown jewels.

"What in heaven's name is that all about?" Sunday exclaimed.

"What do you think, darling?" Henry inquired as he studied it carefully. "Well done, Sims. I think this should handle the job quite adequately."

"Are you planning to saw me in half?" Sunday asked.

"Orson Welles and Rita Hayworth had quite a successful act staging that scene. No, my sweet love, you and I are going into the woods. This morning when I was riding I spotted a magnificent evergreen that will be perfect for our first Christmas tree. It's at the north end of the property, out past the lake."

"You're going to cut it down yourself?" Sunday protested. "Henry, you're taking this 'all-around' business too seriously . . ."

Henry held up his free hand. "No arguments. I heard you say several weeks ago that one of your happiest memories was going out with your father to buy the Christmas tree, then helping him carry it home and trim it. This year, you and I are starting our own tradition."

Sunday tucked a runaway lock of blond hair behind her ear. "You're serious, aren't you?"

"Absolutely. We're going to tramp through the snow into our woods. I am going to cut down the tree, and together we're going to drag it back here."

Henry beamed in satisfaction at his plan. "Tomorrow is Christmas Eve. If we get the tree in and up today, we can start trimming it this evening and finish tomorrow. Sims will bring out the boxes from the storeroom, and you can select any ornaments you choose."

"We have quite a selection, madam," Sims volunteered. "Just last year Lanning decorators came as usual and did the blue-and-silver effect. Quite beautiful. The year before we had a white Christmas. Ah, yes, it was much admired."

"Lanning must be having a heart attack that you're not having him in this year," Sunday observed as she put the files and notepad aside and stood up. She walked over to Henry and put her arms around his waist. "I can see through you. You're doing this for me."

He cupped her face in his hands. "You've had a rough few weeks. I think we're putting together exactly the kind of Christmas you need. All the household help except for Sims gone, the Secret Service guys home with their own families. It'll be just the two of us and Sims."

Sunday swallowed over the sudden lump in her throat. Her mother had had an emergency triple bypass several weeks earlier. She was now recuperating at the Britland estate in the Bahamas, with Sunday's father in attendance.

But it had been touch and go for a while, and the fear of losing her mother had shaken Sunday to the core.

"If it's quite all right with you, madam, that I stay . . ." Sims said, his tone questioning, his voice dignified, his demeanor as always stately.

"Sims, this has been your home for over thirty years," Sunday said. "You bet we want you to stay."

She pointed to the saw. "I thought woodchoppers used axes."

"You get to carry the ax," Henry said. "It's cold out there. Wear your ski outfit."

From behind the thick trunk of a hundred-year-old oak, Jacques cautiously moved his head to observe the tall man cutting down the tree. The lady was laughing and seemed to be trying to help, while the other man, who looked something like *Grand-père,* just stood there.

Jacques didn't want them to see him. They might give him back to Lily, and Lily frightened him. In fact, she had frightened him since she first arrived to baby-sit him while *Maman* and Richard went on their trip.

Maman and Richard had been married last week. Jacques had liked his new daddy a lot, until Lily told him that *Maman* and Richard had phoned to say they didn't want him anymore and had told her to take him away. Then they got in Lily's car and drove for a long time. Jacques remembered that he'd been asleep when a loud noise woke him, and the car spun around, then went off the road. The door next to him flew open, and he ran away.

Why didn't *Maman* give him to *Grand-père* if she didn't want him any longer? *Grand-père* had gone back to Paris earlier today. When he left, *Grand-père* told Jacques how happy he would be living in this nice place called Darien, in Richard's new home. *Grand-père* promised that he could spend a month with him at the country house in Aix-en-Provence next summer, and in the meantime he would be sending Jacques lots of messages on his computer.

Even though he was going to be six soon, and *Maman* kept calling him her "little man," it was too much for Jacques to understand. All he knew was that *Maman* and Richard did not want him, and that he didn't want to be with Lily. If he could just *talk* to *Grand-père*, maybe *Grand-père* would come and get him. But what if *Grand-père* told him he had to stay with Lily? Better not to talk to anyone, Jacques thought.

Opposite him, the big tree came down with a crash. The tall man and the lady and the man who looked like *Grand-père* began to cheer, and then together they took hold of it and started to drag it away.

Silently, Jacques followed them.

"A most satisfactory evergreen, sir," Sims remarked, "but perhaps it could be a trifle more centered."

"It isn't in the stand straight," Sunday observed. "In fact it's slightly lopsided. That's why it looks off center."

She was sitting cross-legged on the floor of the library going through the neatly packed boxes of Christmas ornaments. "However," she added, "considering the energy you two expended getting that tree into the stand in the first place, I'd suggest you leave it alone. It will be fine."

"I fully intend to," Henry said. "Which color scheme are you using?"

"None," Sunday told him. "All mixed up. Real loving-hands-at-home. Multicolored lights. Tinsel. I wish you had some battered ornaments that you remember from the time you were a kid."

"Better than that, I have *your* battered ornaments," Henry told her. "Before your folks left for Nassau, your dad retrieved them for me."

"I shall fetch the box containing them, sir," Sims offered, "and perhaps you and Madam would enjoy a glass of champagne while you decorate your tree."

"Fine with me," Henry said as he rubbed callused palms together. "You're ready for some bubbly, aren't you, sweetheart?"

Sunday did not answer. She was staring out at a spot just past the evergreen. "Henry," she said quietly, "please don't think I'm crazy, but for a second, I thought I saw a child's face pressed against the window."

Richard Dalton glanced briefly at his wife of seven days as they turned off Connecticut's Merritt Parkway and onto the road that led to Darien. In fluent French, he said, "I owe you a real honeymoon, Giselle."

Giselle DuBois Dalton tucked her hand under her husband's arm and answered in accented English. "Remember, Richard, from now on you're supposed to speak only English to me. And don't worry. We'll have a real honeymoon later. You know I wouldn't want to leave Jacques alone with a strange baby-sitter for more than a few hours. He's so shy."

"She speaks fluent French, dear, and that was important. The agency recommended her very highly."

"Even so." Giselle's voice sounded troubled. "Everything was so rushed, wasn't it?"

It *was* rushed, Dalton thought. He and Giselle had planned to be married in May. But the date got moved up when he had been offered the presidency of All-Flav, the worldwide soft drink company. Prior to then, he had been director of Coll-ette, All-Flav's chief competitor's French division. They had agreed that nobody only thirty-four years old turned down that kind of job, especially when it came with a substantial signing bonus. Giselle and he had been married last week and a few days later had come to the house the company rented for them in Darien.

On Friday evening the housekeeper, Lily, who they had been told would not be available to start with them until after Christmas, had unexpectedly shown up. So on Saturday morning, Giselle's father, Louis, urged them to go to New York for a brief honeymoon weekend. "I'll be here with Jacques until noon on Monday. Then Lily can certainly mind him for a few hours until you return Monday afternoon after the company luncheon," he had said.

But the company Christmas luncheon had run longer than expected, and now, as they got nearer to the Darien house, Richard could feel Giselle's tension building.

He understood her concern. Widowed at twenty-four and left with an infant son, she had gone to work in the publicity department of Coll-ette; it was there that they had met a year ago.

It hadn't been an easy courtship. Giselle was so fiercely protective of Jacques, so afraid that a stepfather—any stepfather—wouldn't be good to him.

They also had expected to live in Paris indefinitely. But then, in just a matter of a few weeks, she had to both change her wedding plans and relocate. Richard knew that Giselle's biggest worry, however, was that the change—a new father, a new home—was too abrupt for Jacques. Besides, he was barely starting to learn English.

"Home sweet new home," Richard said cheerfully as he steered the car into the long driveway.

Giselle was opening the passenger door even before he braked.

"The house is so dark," she said. "Why didn't Lily turn the lights on?"

Richard's flip suggestion that Lily was obviously a thrifty French lady died on his lips. The house had a deserted air about it even he found ominous. Although it was almost dark, there wasn't a single light shining from any window.

He caught up with Giselle at the front door. She was fumbling in her purse for her key. "I have it, dear," he told her.

The door opened to reveal a shadowed foyer.

"Jacques," Giselle called. "Jacques."

Richard flicked the light switch. As the area brightened, he saw a sheet of paper propped on the foyer table. It read: *"N'appelez pas la police. Attendez nos instructions avant de rien faire."*

Don't call the police. Wait for instructions.

"Miss LaMonte, how are you feeling?"

She opened her eyes slowly to see a solicitous state trooper looking down at her. What had happened? she wondered briefly. Then vivid memory came flooding back. The car had blown a tire, and she had lost control. It had gone off the road and down the embankment. She had smashed her head on the wheel.

The boy. Jacques. Had he told them about her? What should she say? She would go to prison.

She felt a hand on her shoulder. She realized that a doctor was standing on the other side of the bed.

"Easy," he said reassuringly. "You're in the emergency room of Morristown General Hospital. You've had a pretty bad bump, but otherwise you're fine. We tried to notify your family, but there's no answer yet."

Notify her family? Of course. She still had the card case Pete had lifted, with the real Lily LaMonte's driver's license, registration, medical insurance, and credit cards.

Despite her throbbing head, Betty Rouche's ability to lie returned with lightning speed. "Actually, that's fortunate. I'm joining my family for Christmas, and I wouldn't want to frighten them with a call."

Where should she say she was joining them? *Where was the boy?*

"You were alone in the car?"

A vague impression of the passenger door opening filtered through her clouded memory. The child must have run away. "Yes," she whispered.

"Your car has been towed to the nearest gas station, but I'm afraid it needs major repairs," the state trooper told her. "It may well be a write-off."

She had to get out of here. Betty looked at the doctor. "I'll have my brother come back and take care of the car. Can I leave now?"

"Yes, I would say so. But take it easy. And see your own physician next week."

With a reassuring smile the doctor left the cubicle.

"I'll need you to sign the accident report," the trooper told her. "Will someone pick you up?"

"Yes. Thank you. I'll phone my brother."

"Well, good luck. It could have been a lot worse. A blowout and no air bag . . ." The trooper did not finish the thought.

Ten minutes later, Betty was in a cab on her way to a rental car agency. Twenty minutes after that, she was on her way to New York City. The plan had been to take the boy to her cousin Pete's house in Somerville, but no way was she going there now.

She waited until she was safely out of town before she pulled into a gas station and phoned. Now that she was somewhere safer, she had to vent her fury on the cousin who had talked her into this crazy scheme.

"It's a cinch," he had told her, "the kind of break that comes along once in a lifetime." Pete worked for the Best Choice Employment Agency in Darien. He called himself a trainee, but Betty knew his job ranged from running errands to mowing lawns for the rental properties the agency managed.

Like her, he was thirty-two; they had grown up next door to each other and, over the years, had gotten into a lot of trouble together. They still laughed about how they had trashed the high school, an adventure for which other kids got blamed.

But she should have known Pete was out of his league with this crazy scheme. "Look," he had told her, "at the agency I heard all about them, this couple with the kid. This guy, Richard Dalton, just deposited a check for six million bucks; his signing bonus, they call it. I've even worked at the rental place they'll be living in. Another executive had it six months ago. And I know Lily La-Monte. She's been used by other people through the

agency, and she's the only one they have who is right for
this job. They need a nanny who is fluent in French. Well,
I happen to know she's going to New Mexico for Christmas. So you take her place. You're her type and age, and
you speak good French. Once the couple takes off, you
take the kid to my place in Somerville. I'll handle picking
up the ransom and all that. It'll be a swap. We get a million
bucks to split between us."

"And if they call the cops?"

"They won't, but even if they do, what does it matter?
Nobody knows you. Why suspect me? We won't hurt the
kid. Plus I'll be in a position to watch what's happening.
Part of my job is to keep that place plowed and shoveled.
We're gonna have more snow. So I'll know if there's any
sign of cops there. I phone and tell Dalton to leave the
money in their mailbox tomorrow night and the kid's home
for Christmas. Get the cops and they won't hear from us
again."

"And if they do bring in the cops, what do we do with
the child?"

"Same thing we do if we get the money. No matter what
goes down, you leave the kid in a church in New York.
Their prayers will be answered."

To Betty it sounded like trashing the school and getting
away with it. Pete wouldn't hurt the kid any more than she
would. Just like it never even occurred to them to burn
down the school. They wouldn't have done that.

When he answered the phone, Pete's voice was edgy. "I
thought you'd be in Somerville hours ago."

"I might have been if you'd made sure that lousy car
had decent tires," Betty snapped.

"What's that supposed to mean?"

She could feel her voice rising as she told him what had happened.

He interrupted her. "Shut up and listen to me. The deal's off. Forget the money. No more contact with them. Where's the kid?"

"I don't know. I woke up in a hospital. Apparently the boy had run off before the cops found me."

"If he starts talking, they'll tie him to you. Do they know you were renting another car?"

"The cabdriver knows."

"Okay. Dump that car and get lost. Just make sure you lie low. Remember, there's nothing to tie us to the missing kid."

"Sure there isn't," Betty exclaimed bitterly as she slammed down the phone.

"Sir, there's no report as yet of a missing child," the policeman told Henry. "But I'll take the boy to headquarters; a representative of Family Services will pick him up there if no one comes for him soon. Chances are, though, that some mighty worried people are searching hard for him right now."

They were clustered in the library at Drumdoe. The room was dominated by the towering, still-unadorned, slightly-tilted Christmas tree, which remained exactly as it had been when Sunday spotted Jacques's face at the window. Realizing he had been seen, the little boy had tried to run away, but Henry had rushed out in time to catch him. When their gentle questions yielded nothing but silence, Henry had phoned the police while Sunday unzipped and removed the child's outer jacket. Gently she had rubbed warmth back into chilled small fingers, all the while keeping up a steady stream of words, hoping to win his confidence, heartsick to see the terror in his blue-green eyes.

Now the policeman squatted in front of the child. "About five or six, wouldn't you think, sir? That's what my sister's kid is, and he's about this size." He smiled at Jacques. "I'm a policeman and I'm going to help find your mom and dad. Bet they're looking all over the place for you right now. We're going to go for a ride in my car to the place where they can pick you up. Okay?"

He put his hand on Jacques's shoulder and started to ease the boy toward him. His face contorted with fear, Jacques pulled back and turned toward Sunday, grabbing her skirt with both hands as though begging for protection.

"He's frightened to death," Sunday said. She knelt beside the quivering boy and put her arm around him. "Officer, can't you just leave him here? I'm sure you'll get a call about him soon. While we're waiting, he can help us trim the tree. Can't you, little guy?"

Sunday felt the small boy shrinking against her. "Can't you?" she asked gently. At his lack of response, she said, "I think he may not be able to hear."

"Or speak," Henry agreed. "Officer, I think my wife is right. You know he's safe and warm here. We'll give him dinner; certainly by then you'll have learned who he is and where he belongs."

"I'm afraid I can't do that, sir. I will have to take him to headquarters. We'll need to take his picture and have an exact physical description for the teletype alert we'll send out. Then it will be up to the Family Services people to decide if we can place him with you until he's claimed."

* * *

Maman had taught him a long time ago that if he ever got lost, he should go to a *gendarme* and tell him his name and his address and his phone number. Jacques was sure that this man was a *gendarme*, but he couldn't give him his name or address or phone number. *Maman* and Richard had given him away to Lily, and he didn't want her to come for him, ever.

This lady reminded him of *Maman*. Her hair was the same color and the way she smiled at him was the way *Maman* smiled. She was gentle. Not like Lily, who did not smile, and who made him change into the uncomfortably tight clothes he was wearing now. Jacques was hungry and tired. And very afraid. He wanted to be back in Paris, safe with *Maman* and *Grand-père*.

Soon it would be *la Fête de Noël*. Last year Richard had come to their house with trains for him. Jacques remembered that together they had laid the tracks and set up the train station and the bridges and the little houses along the tracks. Richard had promised they would set them up this year in the new house. But Richard had lied to him.

Jacques felt himself being picked up. They were going to take him away, back to Lily. In terror, he buried his face in his hands.

Two hours later, when Lily had not appeared, and the *gendarme* brought him back to the big house, Jacques felt the scared feeling start to go away. He knew Lily wasn't in this house. He would be safe here. Tears of relief welled in his eyes. The door opened, and the man who looked like *Grand-père* let them in and led them back to the room with the Christmas tree. The tall man and the lady were there.

"The child was examined," the policeman told Henry

and Sunday. "The doctor says he's in good health and seems to have been well cared for. He still hasn't spoken, and he refused to eat anything, but the doctor says it's too soon to tell if it's a physical problem or if he's just frightened. We have his picture and description on the teletype. My guess is that he'll be claimed pretty soon, but in the meantime Family Services okayed his staying with you."

Jacques did not know what the *gendarme* had said, but the lady who looked like *Maman* knelt down and put her arms around him. He could tell she was kind; he felt safe with her, a little like the way he had felt when *Maman* had loved him. The giant lump in his throat began to melt.

Sunday felt him tremble against her. "It's okay to cry," she murmured, as she stroked his silky brown hair.

Richard Dalton watched helplessly as his wife sat staring at the phone. Giselle was clearly in shock. Her pupils were enormous, her face expressionless. As the hours passed and they heard nothing from Jacques's kidnappers, his every instinct insisted that the police be called. But at the suggestion, Giselle became almost hysterical. *"Non, non, non,* you cannot, you will not. They will kill him. We must do what they say. We must wait for instructions."

He should have known something was wrong when that woman showed up unexpectedly, he told himself bitterly. The agency had been adamant that she would be away over Christmas and could not begin working until the twenty-seventh. We should have checked, of course, he thought. It would have been simple just to call the agency and confirm. But how did the woman who had said she was Lily LaMonte know to come to the house? Obviously it had all been planned; she was to abduct Jacques at the first opportunity. It was Giselle's father who had finally convinced them to accept the woman who called herself Lily LaMonte, and who urged them to spend the weekend in New York. It was ironic as well, for he would be distraught if anything happened to Jacques. No, it was not his fault, Richard thought. We probably would have entrusted Jacques to that woman today when we went to the company luncheon. He shook his head. Maybe, maybe not, he thought. It's too late to wonder about such things now.

He had to do *something* though. The inactivity was driving him crazy. He had to believe that this was about money and that they would get Jacques back by tomorrow.

Tomorrow.

Christmas Eve!

He sighed. Maybe it wouldn't be that quick. His signing bonus had been well publicized. It was logical for the kidnapper to assume that he could put his hands on six million dollars. But surely no one would expect that he would have that kind of money available at short notice. The most he could get from a cash machine was a few hundred dollars.

The kidnapper or kidnappers had to be planning to keep Jacques overnight. If they phoned by morning, he would be able to get cash from the bank. But how much cash? How much would they demand? If it was in the millions, it would take several days to get it together. No bank had that much ready cash on tap. And large withdrawals meant questions.

Giselle was weeping now, tears that slid silently down her cheeks. Her lips were forming her son's name. *Jacques. Jacques.*

It's my fault, Richard thought. Giselle and Jacques came

with me willingly, and look what I've done to them. He could not stand the inactivity any longer. He had promised Jacques that they would set up his trains in time for Christmas. He looked about the room. The boxes were in a corner of the family room in which they were sitting.

Richard got up, went over to the boxes, and squatted on the floor. His strong fingers ripped the seal of the first box apart, and he reached in and pulled out sections of track. Last year, on Christmas Eve, when Jacques opened the brightly wrapped packages in *Grand-père's* house, Richard had explained that Santa had left this present early so that he could help Jacques put it together. When the tracks and the trains and the bridges and the houses were completely set up, he had pointed out the switch to Jacques.

"This is what makes it start," he had explained. "Try it."

Jacques had thrown the switch. The lights in the little houses blazed, the whistles blew, the crossing gates came down, and as he cautiously opened the throttle, the antique Lionel locomotive with six cars behind it chugged for a few moments, then raced forward.

The look of awe on Jacques's face had been indescribable.

Come on, Jacques, Richard prayed, I'm going to put this train set together again, and you've got to get back here to run it with me.

The phone rang. He jumped up, managing to take it from Giselle's grasp before she had a chance to speak. "Richard Dalton," he said crisply.

A voice, low and husky, obviously attempting to be disguised, asked, "How much cash you got in the house?"

Richard thought rapidly. "About two thousand dollars," he said.

Pete Schuler had changed his mind. Maybe he could get a few bucks out of this after all.

"Did you call the police?"

"No, I swear we didn't."

"Okay. Leave the cash in the mailbox now. Then close all the blinds. I don't want you looking out, understand?"

"Yes, yes. We'll do anything you say. Is Jacques all right? I want to talk to him."

"You'll talk to him soon enough. Put the cash out where I told you and the kid is trimming the tree with you tomorrow night."

"Take care of him. You've got to take care of him."

"We will. But remember, any sign of police and he's in South America being adopted. Got it?"

They haven't threatened to kill him, Richard thought. At least they haven't threatened to kill him. Then he heard a click. He put the phone down and put his arms around Giselle. "He'll be returned to us tomorrow," he said.

The window of the second-floor center bedroom looked out directly over the curbside mailbox. It was at this window that Richard established his observation post, peering through a slit in the draperies. The phone, on a long extension cord, was positioned right next to him. He knew that Giselle might not understand any instructions the growly voiced caller would give. Clearly, she was on the verge of collapse, but he did manage to get her to lie on the bed near the window, an afghan tucked around her. His final preparation had been to adjust his camera to allow for the minimal lighting conditions.

As he settled in for his watch, Richard realized despairingly how little he would be able to learn about anyone who attempted to take the money. The street was unlighted, the sky filled with heavy, threatening clouds. He would be lucky to even determine the make of car the person was driving. *I should call the police*, he thought. That's probably the one chance we would have to follow whoever comes here for the money.

He sighed. But if he *did* notify the police, and then something went wrong, he would never be able to forgive himself, and he knew that Giselle would never forgive him.

His mind flashed back to when he was nine years old, and to the piano lessons his mother had made him take. One of the few songs he had managed to get through without a mistake was "All Through the Night." He remembered that his mother would sometimes sit beside him on the piano bench and sing the words while he played:

> Sleep, my child, and peace attend thee
> All through the night.
> Guardian angels God will send thee
> All through the night.

Let guardian angels take care of our little boy, Richard prayed silently as he listened to Giselle's soft sobbing.

A final fragment of the song ran through his head: *"And I my loving vigil keeping, all through the night."*

Dinner was simple: salad, French bread, pasta with basil and tomato sauce. The child sat with Henry and Sunday at the table in the small dining room. He took the napkin from beside the plate and placed it on his lap, but did not look at Sims when offered the bread and did not touch the food.

"He *has* to be hungry," Henry said. "It's nearly seven-thirty." He took a bite of the pasta and smiled at Jacques. "Ummm . . . delicious."

Jacques looked at him gravely, then averted his eyes.

"Perhaps a peanut-butter-and-jelly sandwich?" Sims suggested. "How you enjoyed them when you were a lad, sir."

"Let's just ignore him for a few minutes and see what happens," Sunday said. "I think he's terribly frightened, but I agree, he must be hungry. If he doesn't start eating in a couple of minutes, we'll switch menus. Sims, if we do try the peanut-butter-and-jelly sandwich, substitute milk for the Coke."

She twirled pasta onto her fork. "Henry, don't you think it's very odd that the police haven't heard from anyone about a missing child? I mean, if he were from a house around here, any normal parent would have been calling them immediately to report him missing. My point is, how did he *get* here? Do you think he might have been deliber-ately left on our doorstep?"

"I can't believe that," Henry said. "Anyone deliber-ately planning to leave the child here would have to be psychic to know that we sent the Secret Service guys home for these few days. Otherwise they'd have been seen and questioned at the gates. I think it's more likely that for some incredible reason he simply hasn't been missed yet."

Sunday glanced at Jacques then quickly back at Henry. "Don't look now," she said quietly, "but a certain little guy is starting to dig in."

For the rest of the meal, she and Henry chatted, ostensibly ignoring Jacques, who finished the entire plate of pasta, the salad, and the Coke.

Sunday noticed him eyeing the bread, which was out of his reach. Casually she nudged the basket nearer to him. "Another observation," she said. "He wanted the bread but couldn't ask for it, and wouldn't reach for it. Henry, this child, whether you realize it or not, has very good table manners."

After dinner, they went back to the library to finish trimming the tree. Sunday pointed out the last full box of ornaments to Jacques, and he began handing them to her. She noticed how careful he was as he plucked them, one by one, from the cardboard separators. That's something else he's done before, she decided. Later she noticed that his eyes were beginning to droop.

When the last ornament was taken from the box and hung on the tree, she said, "I think somebody needs to go to bed. The question is, where do we put him?"

"Darling, there are at least sixteen bedrooms in this house."

"Yes, but where did you sleep when you were this guy's size?"

"In the nursery suite."

"With your nanny nearby?"

"Of course."

"Exactly."

Sims was piling the empty boxes together. "Sims, I think we'll put our little friend on the couch in our sitting room," Sunday said. "That way we can leave the bedroom door open and he can see and hear us."

"Very good, madam. As to nightdress?"

"One of Henry's tee shirts will do fine."

Later that night, Sunday awakened to a faint stirring from the next room. In an instant she was out of bed, across the carpet, and at the door of the adjacent sitting room.

Jacques was standing at the window, his face raised to the sky. A faint drone caught her attention. A plane was passing overhead. He must have heard it, she thought. I wonder what it means to him.

As she watched, the little boy walked back to the couch, got under the covers and buried his face in the pillow.

Christmas Eve dawned crisp and bright. A dusting of predawn snow left a glittery, fresh surface on already white lawns and fields. Henry, Sunday, and Jacques went for an early morning walk.

"Darling, you do know we can't keep him indefinitely," Henry said. A deer ran through the woods, and Jacques rushed ahead of them to witness its swift flight.

"I know, Henry."

"You were right to keep him near us last night. I think I'm starting to realize what it will be like when we have children of our own, sweetheart. Will they *all* sleep on the couch in the sitting room?"

Sunday laughed. "No, but they won't be in another wing of the house, either. Have you finished your Christmas greeting for the Internet?"

"Yes, I have. So many people from all over the world wrote to us this year that I think it's an appropriate time to convey our good wishes and gratitude to them."

"I do too." Then Sunday's voice changed. "Henry, look!"

Jacques had abruptly stopped running and now stood looking up longingly at the sky.

They could hear the drone of an airplane far above. "Henry," Sunday said slowly, "another clue: I think that little boy has recently been on a plane."

Pete Schuler was not comforted by the realization that he had two thousand, three hundred and thirty-three bucks in his pocket, even though the windfall did mean that he could take the rest of the winter off and go ski somewhere. Several questions still nagged at him.

Where was the kid? Why didn't he show up? His dumb cousin, Betty, had lost him somewhere in New Jersey. How come some nice, concerned citizen hadn't found him and turned him over to the cops? Suppose the kid had had an accident? He turned the questions over in his mind, his nerves jumping.

Betty was at her friend's pad in New York, that dump in the East Village. Pete dialed the number. Betty answered. Her voice was ragged. "The kid back home yet?" she asked.

"No. Where the hell did you lose him?"

"Bernardsville. That was the name of the town. Do you think he got run over or something?"

"How am I supposed to know? You're the one who lost him." Pete hesitated, considering. "I'm pretty sure the parents haven't called the police." He wasn't about to tell Betty that he had gotten any money. "But we need to know what's going on. Just in case they have some kind of tracer on him, you take a bus over to New Jersey, call the Bernardsville police from a phone booth, and ask if a five-year-old kid was turned in to them. Got it?"

"What good will that do? What do you think they'll tell me?" Betty asked. *Why did I get into this?* she was thinking. If something has happened to this kid, I could go to jail for the rest of my life.

"Do it. Now! But be careful. If they have the kid they'll ask you a bunch of questions," Pete snapped.

At two o'clock, Betty called him back. "I'm not sure if they have him or not," she said. "They asked me to describe the child. I hung up fast."

"That was stupid," Pete told her curtly. He broke the connection. If the Daltons hadn't yet gone to the police, it was a sure thing they would very soon, especially if they didn't get further word from him. He drove to a gas station in Southport, and shut himself in the phone booth. He would have to make the next move himself.

The phone was answered on the first ring. "Richard Dalton."

"There's been a delay," Schuler said in the same semi-disguised voice he had attempted before, speaking through a handkerchief over the mouthpiece, the way he had seen it done in the movies. "Just don't panic. Got it? *Don't panic!*"

Richard Dalton heard the click as the caller hung up. Something *has* gone wrong, he thought. Whoever had taken the money came on foot, he realized. *That* was why he hadn't seen anyone. All night long he had stayed awake, watching for a car to drive down the block. It hadn't come. Still, in the morning the money was gone. Somehow he had completely missed the person who had taken it.

The phone rang again. Dalton grabbed it, identified himself, listened, then covered the mouthpiece with his hand. "It's your father," he said, "he wants to speak to Jacques."

"Tell him Jacques and I are out, doing our last-minute Christmas shopping," Giselle whispered. Her face was a mask of fear and pain. Richard could hardly bear to look into her eyes.

"Louis, they're out shopping," Richard said. "We'll surely speak with you tomorrow."

As he replaced the receiver, Giselle screamed, "Tell him that Jacques and I are Christmas shopping."

She fell to the floor in a faint, accidentally hitting the switch for the electric train. The lights blazed on, the crossing gates went down, the locomotive chugged, then roared.

Dalton strode across the room, snapped off the switch, then cradled his wife in his arms.

At five o'clock on Christmas Eve, the police chief of Bernardsville phoned and asked to speak to Henry. "Mr. President," he said, "there are flyers being distributed in all the neighboring areas about the boy. The FBI field office and all fifty states have his picture and description. We've checked with the National Center for Missing and Exploited Children. So far, we're drawing a complete blank. I can tell you though, that we did get one odd phone call today, asking if a five-year-old boy had been turned in to us. This is beginning to look like an abandoned child situation. Has he said anything yet?"

"Not a word," Henry admitted.

"Then we think it best if we take custody of the boy. We need to take him to the hospital and have him evaluated properly to see if he really can't speak, or if perhaps he's been traumatized."

"Hold on, Chief, please."

Sunday had sent Sims to the local Toys-R-Us, and he had returned laden with gifts. Most of the presents were still wrapped. They had opened a few, however, including a large box of heavy plastic interlocking building blocks, with which she and Jacques were constructing an elaborate tower. She listened with dismay as Henry repeated the message. "Henry, it's Christmas Eve. This little boy can't wake up in a hospital tomorrow."

"And we can't keep him indefinitely, darling."

"Tell them to leave him with us until Thursday. At least let him have Christmas. He's comfortable here, I know he is. And something else, Henry. Sims bought some new clothes. The stuff he was wearing appears new but doesn't fit him. There's something strange going on. I don't think he was abandoned; I think his family doesn't know where to look for him. Tell the police that."

Jacques did not know what the nice lady who looked a little like *Maman* was saying. He *did* know that he was glad to be with her, as well as with the nice tall man and the old man who looked like *Grand-père*. Maybe if he was a very good boy they would let him stay with them. But he also wanted to be home with *Maman* and Richard. Why had they sent him away? Suddenly he couldn't hold the sadness in any longer. He put down the small block he was about to place on the very top of the tower and began to cry—silent, hopeless, lonely tears that even the nice lady who rocked him in her arms could not prevent.

That night he could not eat dinner. He really tried, but

the food wouldn't go down his throat. Later they went back into the room with the Christmas tree, and all he could think about was the train set he and Richard were going to put together in the new house in Darien.

Sunday knew what Henry was thinking. They weren't really helping the little boy. He was grieving, a silent, persistent grief that all the toys in the world wouldn't help. Maybe he did belong in a hospital where he could get professional help.

She experienced the same helpless feeling she had had when she waited with Henry and her father during her mother's operation.

"What are you thinking, love?" Henry asked quietly.

"Just that we'd better let the professionals take over tomorrow. You were right. We're not doing him any favors keeping him here."

"I agree."

"It doesn't feel much like Christmas Eve," Sunday said sadly. "A lost child . . . I can't believe someone isn't looking for him. Can you imagine how we'd feel if *our* little boy were missing?"

Henry started to answer, then tilted his head. "Listen. The Christmas carolers are coming."

He crossed to the window and opened it. As the crisp air blew into the room, the carolers drew nearer to the house. They were singing "God Rest You, Merry Gentlemen."

Let nothing you dismay, Sunday thought. Softly she hummed with them as they switched to the familiar poignant words of "Silent Night."

She and Henry applauded, as the group launched into "Deck the Halls with Boughs of Holly."

Then the leader of the carolers approached the window and said, "Mr. President, we learned a special song for you because we read once that it was a favorite of yours at school. If we may . . ."

He blew on the pitch pipe and the group softly began to sing,

> *"Un flambeau, Jeannette Isabelle,*
> *Un flambeau, courrons au berceau.*
> *C'est Jésus, bonnes gens du hameau*
> *Le Christ est né. . . ."*

From behind her, Sunday heard a sound. Jacques had remained hunched on the chair opposite the couch, where they had been sitting when the carolers had appeared. As she watched, he bolted upright. His half-closed eyes opened wide. His lips moved in synch with the singers'.

"Henry," she said quietly, "look. Do you see what I see?"

Henry turned. "What do you mean, darling?"

"Look!"

Without seeming to study Jacques, Henry stared at him intently. "He *knows* that song." He went over and scooped the little boy up in his arms.

"Again, please," he requested when the carolers stopped. But when they sang the song again, Jacques sealed his lips.

When the carolers had left, Henry turned to the little boy and began speaking French. *"Comment t'appelles-tu? Où habites-tu?"*

But Jacques only closed his eyes.

Henry looked at Sunday and shrugged. "I don't know

what else to do. He won't answer me, but I think he understands what I'm asking."

Sunday looked thoughtfully at Jacques. "Henry, you must have noticed how fascinated our little friend was when a plane flew overhead this afternoon."

"You pointed it out to me."

"And the same thing happened last night. Henry, suppose this child just got here from another country. No wonder he hasn't been reported missing. Sims brought back one of the flyers with his picture and description, didn't he?"

"Yes."

"Henry. You were going to put a Christmas greeting on the Internet, weren't you?"

"My annual message. Yes. At midnight."

"Henry, do me a favor." Sunday pointed to Jacques. "This year put the flyer with his picture and description on as well, and especially ask people in France and other French-speaking countries to take particular note of his picture. And from now on, talk to me in French. I may not get much of it, but maybe we'll make a breakthrough."

It was quarter of six in the morning in Paris when Louis de Coyes, his coffee in hand, went into his study and turned on the computer. Christmas morning alone was an unhappy prospect. At least later he would join friends for Christmas dinner. The house was lonely without Jacques and Giselle, but Louis was well satisfied with his daughter's choice of a husband. Richard Dalton was the kind of man any father would like to see his daughter marry.

And they would visit a great deal, he was confident of that. They had promised that the lessons he had begun to give Jacques on the Internet would be continued. Someday before too long, he and his grandson would be able to communicate regularly by E-mail. In the meantime, it was now almost midnight on the east coast of the United States, and he wanted to read the Christmas message that Henry Parker Britland IV was about to send to his well-wishers. Louis had once met the former President at a reception at the American embassy in Paris and had been impressed by his ready wit and genuine warmth.

Five minutes later, an incredulous Louis de Coyes was staring at the picture of his grandson, whom the former president had described as a missing child.

Six minutes later, Richard Dalton, while preparing to form some excuse for Giselle not coming to the phone to speak to her father, was shouting, "Oh my God, Louis, oh my God."

At 2:00 A.M. the bell rang. Henry and Sunday were waiting for Jacques's parents. "He's asleep upstairs."

Jacques was having a dream, but this time, it was a very good dream. *Maman* was kissing him and whispering, *"Mon petit, mon Jacques, mon Jacques, je t'aime, je t'aime."*

Jacques felt himself being lifted up, blankets tucked around him. Richard was holding him tight, was saying, "Little boy, we're going home."

In the dream, Jacques slept in *Maman*'s arms in a car for a long time.

When he awoke, he opened his eyes slowly, the sad feeling creeping over him. But he was not on a couch in the big house. He was in his own bed. How did he get here? Was the dream not a dream after all? Had *Maman* and Richard come for him because they loved him?

"*Maman!* Richard!" Jacques called eagerly as he hopped out of bed and ran into the hallway.

"Down here, Jacques," *Maman* called. And then he heard another sound floating up from downstairs. The chug-chugging of his trains, and the whistle blowing for the gates to lower. Jacques's eager feet barely touched the stairs as he rushed down them.

"Not much sleep last night," Henry observed as he and Sunday drove home from church.

"Nope, not much," Sunday agreed happily. "Henry, I'm going to miss that little guy."

"So am I. But before too long I expect we'll have one —or two—of our own."

"I hope so. But isn't it incredible how fragile life is? I mean that call about my mother last month?"

"She's doing fine."

"Yes, but we could have lost her. And little Jacques. Suppose that woman who took him hadn't had the accident right here in town. God only knows if she wouldn't have panicked and maybe hurt him. I hope they catch her soon. We do all hang by a thread."

"Yes, we do," Henry agreed quietly. "And for some of us, that thread is going to be cut very soon. Don't worry, the police won't have a problem finding that woman and her accomplice. Both were apparently clumsy about covering their trails."

They drove through the open gates of Drumdoe and down the long road to the house. Henry parked the car in front of the steps. Sims had obviously been watching for them, because the door opened as they crossed the porch.

"Little Jacques is on the phone, sir. His mother tells me he has been playing all morning with his trains. He wishes to thank you for your goodness to him." Sims beamed. "He wishes to offer you a *joyeux Noël.*"

As Henry hurried to the phone, Sunday grinned at Sims. "Your French accent is almost as lousy as mine," she said.

THE QUEEN OF SUSPENSE

MARY HIGGINS CLARK

#1
New York Times
Bestselling
Author

YOU BELONG TO ME

Coming soon from Simon & Schuster

SIMON & SCHUSTER

1438